9/20

ALSO BY HELEN FROST

Keesha's House

Spinning Through the Universe

The Braid

Diamond Willow

Crossing Stones

Hidden

Salt: A Story of Friendship in a Time of War

Room 214: A Year in Poems

When My Sister Started Kissing

all HE knew

all
HE
knew

HELEN FROST

Farrar Straus Giroux • New York

Farrar Straus Giroux Books for Young Readers
An imprint of Macmillan Publishing Group, LLC
120 Broadway, New York, NY 10271

Printed in the United States of America by LSC Communications, Harrisonburg,
Virginia
Designed by Cassie Gonzales
First edition, 2020
10 9 8 7 6 5 4 3 2 1

mackids.com

Library of Congress Cataloging-in-Publication Data

Names: Frost, Helen, 1949– author.
Title: All he knew / Helen Frost.
Description: First edition. | New York: Farrar Straus Giroux Books for Young
    Readers, 2020. | Audience: Ages 10–14. | Audience: Grades 4–6. | Summary:
    In 1939 six-year-old Henry, who is deaf, is taken from his family and placed in a
    home for the feeble-minded where, years later, his friends include a conscientious
    objector serving there during World War II. Includes historical notes.
Identifiers: LCCN 2019033347 | ISBN 9780374312992 (hardcover) |
    ISBN 9780374313005 (ebook)
Subjects: CYAC: Novels in verse. | Inmates of institutions—Fiction. | Deaf—Fiction. |
    People with disabilities—Fiction. | Conscientious objectors—Fiction.
Classification: LCC PZ7.5.F76 All 2020 | DDC [Fic]—dc23
LC record available at https://lccn.loc.gov/2019033347

ISBN 978-0-374-31299-2 (hardcover) / ISBN 978-0-374-31300-5 (ebook)

Our books may be purchased in bulk for promotional, educational, or business use. Please
contact your local bookseller or the Macmillan Corporate and Premium Sales Department
at (800) 221-7945 ext. 5442 or by email at MacmillanSpecialMarkets@macmillan.com.

Dedicated to the memory of
Maxine Sowers Thompson
and her brother
Shirley Sowers
and to her children,
Margaret, Jane, Sarah, Chad

Birds fly here without any sound,
unfolding their wings across the open.

—William Stafford

TABLE OF CONTENTS

all HE Knew

PART I

UNTEACHABLE

1933–1942

ARRIVAL AT RIVERVIEW

SEPTEMBER 1939

Henry comes here on a Greyhound bus.
Slow, along the bumpy road, his mother
in the seat beside him, sitting straight
and tall, her nostrils pinched, her words
held deep inside. She understands by now
that Henry cannot hear them.

Henry is thinking about his sister, Molly.
Why was she trying so hard not to cry, and crying
anyway, when she hugged me this morning?
Papa didn't cry, of course. He never does.
He waved his hand as the bus rolled away,
and Henry, looking out, waved back.

Henry tells himself: *Remember this whole trip.*
Starting at home—the post office, the big old oak tree
on the corner, the water tower, two white churches.
Then out of town—past fields where cows and horses
graze, and other fields where farmers pitch hay
into their wagons. Another town. A city.

More farms. Two more small towns. Henry
tries hard to remember every turn. He feels
so far from home. *How long,* he wonders,

will we be gone this time? Last time
Mama took him on the bus, he hated that place
where a man tried to make him blow out candles.

It wasn't even anybody's birthday, and then the man
got mad when Henry wouldn't do it. That time
it was night when he and Mama got back home.
Papa met them at the bus station, waiting with Molly
in the dark. No one cried that time. So why *was* Molly
crying when he got on the bus this morning?

Henry keeps thinking about that. Maybe those big boys
have been teasing her again. Why do they do that?
Henry thinks it is because of him—the way
those kids pointed at him and said something to Molly.
She stood up tall, as if they couldn't hurt her, then
grabbed Henry's hand and took him home.

Later on, her eyes were red. Henry picked a big bouquet
of dandelions and they brought her smile back.
He wants to get home soon so he can pick more flowers.

Henry brings his mind back to today, concentrates
to make sure he remembers the last few minutes
of the bus ride. The bus stopping every so often
to let people off and on. Then Mama looking at her map
at every stop. Henry thinks:

I bet that barn used to be red when it was new,
but now look how the roof is falling in.
There must be mice in there, because that cat
that just came out is fat.

At the next stop, right after the barn,
Mama gestures,
    Here's where we get off.
The gate. The grounds. A row of trees.
Mama holding out her hand.
Henry's small hand wrapped in hers.

Along the stony path
and up
the twenty-seven stairs.
To this room, where they wait—
blue carpet, big soft chairs. Cool water
in a pitcher, with two drinking glasses.

The heavy door.
The room where Mama
signs some papers.
Back in the first room, a father
arrives with three children
and departs with two.

Henry waits with Mama
until someone comes—a woman,
not unkind. Not gentle, either.
Follow me, she says,
and when she sees he cannot hear,
she points, and Henry walks that way.

Through another door.
Mama not allowed
to follow.
> *Why not?*
> *What is this place?*
> *Who are these people?*

ALL MIXED TOGETHER

A long dark corridor.
Smells he cannot name.
Something like when Granddad
forgot to change his clothes.
Something like the mess
the neighbor's puppy made
before it learned to go outdoors.
Something like potatoes
forgotten in a corner of the kitchen.
All mixed together. Henry tries
to hold his breath, tries
breathing through his mouth—
but then he tastes what he can't
stand to smell. He wants home,
biscuits warming in the oven,
wild roses by the gatepost,
the wind-smell when Mama
takes the sheets down off the line.

What is Molly doing at home right now?
Who will make her smile if I am not there?

MOLLY REMEMBERS HENRY'S FIRST SIX YEARS

1. HENRY IS BORN
JULY 1933

Molly's first memory of Henry:
    Papa didn't have a job,
        so he was home that day.
That was good, because he could help
    Mama when she couldn't lift
        a basket full of peaches.
But it was bad because they didn't have
    money for cloth and thread and buttons
        when they needed new clothes.
They couldn't buy food from the grocery store
    if the hens stopped laying and their
        garden vegetables weren't ready yet.

Molly asked Papa, *Why is Mama*
    in her nightgown in the daytime?
        but before he answered, a neighbor lady,
Mrs. Grayson, who was there to help,
    looked at Molly, cleared her throat, and said,
        She's only five. Molly tried to argue,
I'm five and a half, but Mama said:
    Molly. And then, to Papa,
        Please take her for a walk.
So Papa did.

When they got back, there was a baby,
　　eyes wide open, looking up from a cradle
　　　next to Mama's bed.

Look who's here, said Mama. *Molly,*
　　come and meet your brother,
　　　Henry.

2. HENRY LEARNS TO WALK
JULY 1934

Six days after he was one year old,
    Henry pulled himself up on Molly's chair
        and smiled. She kissed his forehead,
kept on saying, *You can do it, Henry.*
    And he'd say,
        Oo it, Enny.

At last, he let go, took five steps,
    wobbled a little bit, and plopped
        down on the floor.
Henry laughed out loud, and Molly
    helped him get back on his feet
        and do it all again.

3. HENRY'S FEVER
DECEMBER 1937

Molly was almost ten,
    Henry four and a half,
        that Christmas Eve.
They had made presents for each other,
    and those were underneath the tree.
        Molly showed Henry how to tell
which ones were for him, and which
    were hers. He could see the difference
        between *H* and *M*, and he learned
that *H* meant Henry.
    They stayed up late, singing "Jingle Bells,"
        "Joy to the World," and "Silent Night."

Then Henry said, *I don't feel good,*
    and his face was red and hot,
        so Mama sent them both to bed.
Molly drifted off and started dreaming,
    but the sound of Henry crying woke her up
        and she could not get back to sleep.

In the morning, she was mad that Santa hadn't come,
    only the doctor with his big black bag,
        who told them Henry had to stay in bed.

Mama and Papa sat with Henry
    all that day,
        and on through the next night.
He kept calling out:
    Papa! Mama!
        My ears hurt!
After four days and nights,
    Henry started feeling better.
        He got up and had breakfast.
Then Papa remembered about Christmas,
    and called to Molly and Henry—
        Come and open presents.
Molly jumped right up—but Henry didn't.
    Henry, come on! Molly said.
        What? he asked, and she repeated,
Come on!
    It's time to open presents!
        Henry sat there,
staring at her. Finally, she took his arm
    and pulled him to the living room,
        where Papa had the presents.

They each got one store-bought present:
    a jump rope for Molly,
        a harmonica for Henry.

Molly started jumping rope, right there in the house,
    while Papa played a tune on the harmonica,
        trying to show Henry how to do it.

Henry was happy, but he looked confused.
   He said, *Thank you, Papa. It's just like Mr. Grayson's,*
      except his makes sounds when you blow into the holes.

Henry's harmonica *was* making sounds—
   they stopped what they were doing
      and looked at him,
         then at each other.

Papa asked some questions,
   and Henry shook his head. Mama
      had a scared look on her face. She
started singing "Jingle Bells," and Molly
   joined right in,
      but Henry didn't.

Henry could see that people's mouths were moving,
   he could feel his own mouth making words,
      but it sounded to Henry like everyone
was speaking
   from another room
      with the door closed.

That was when Henry and his family
   found out
      that Henry couldn't hear.

4. MOLLY KEPT ON TALKING

JULY 1938

Henry turned five, and Molly tried
    to imagine his silent world.
        No barking dogs? No thunder?
No blue jays squawking at the sparrows?
    If he bit into an apple,
        would he hear a crunching sound?
In wintertime, would he know
    that feeling, when the world gets quiet
        just before it starts to snow?
Molly thought about how Mama called them in
    when it was time for lunch, and how,
        if a car came down the road,
they knew to jump out of the way.
    Now, even if cars honked their horns,
        Henry didn't know it.
She kept her brother close beside her.
    She wondered: *Can Henry hear his own voice*
        when he talks? Is your voice inside your head,
or outside near your ears? She noticed
    that when Henry saw her talking,
        he'd stand in front of her, watching
her face. She learned to stand
    where he could see her mouth move,
        and she spoke slowly, one word at a time,

trying to help him understand.

    Sometimes Henry could.

        Sometimes not.

5. FOR A WHILE, HE TALKED

At first, he talked as much as ever,
    to Mama and Papa and to Molly.
        For a while, he talked to people
in the grocery store or on the street.
    A lot of times, they didn't know
        he couldn't hear them,
and they talked to Henry, too.
    He tried to guess what they were saying—
        usually *Hello* or *Good morning* was enough
of a reply, and then he smiled and walked on.
    But Henry *couldn't* hear the words he spoke,
        and his voice started changing.
Sometimes it was hard to understand him.
    Molly, scared that he'd stop talking,
        kept chattering away to Henry,
even after almost
    everybody else
        had stopped.

6. HENRY DECIDES WHO HE WILL TALK TO

JULY 1939

When Henry turned six, Mama said,
    Let's invite a few children
        to a birthday party. There were three
of them, two girls and a boy,
    and Henry couldn't wait.
        He'd never had a birthday party.

The day arrived, and the boys came first.
    They just said, *Happy birthday, Henry,*
        picked up a ball, and started playing catch.
They didn't try to talk much,
    which was fine with Henry.
        But the girl—Sadie—talked a lot!
Happy birthday, Henry, she began.
    She said it loud and slow, and Henry guessed
        that one easily. *Thank you, Sadie,* he replied.

But then Sadie got excited and started talking fast:
    My mother asked your mother if we
    could make a cake for you, and she said yes!
    I thought you'd like white frosting better,
    but my mother said it should be yellow.
    So that's what we made. Is that okay?

Henry smiled back at Sadie. He could see
there was a question at the end, but he
wasn't sure what she was asking.
I like cake, he guessed.
He could tell from Sadie's face
that wasn't right, but he didn't have
another guess, so he turned to the boys
and said, *Sadie, let's play catch with them.*
One of the boys said, *No girls allowed.*
Since Henry didn't hear that, he had no idea
why Sadie stomped off with her arms crossed.
Come back, he said, but the other boys said,
Let the baby go,
and *Girls can't throw.*

Everyone was mad except for Henry—
he felt like it must be his fault,
but he did not know why.
Then Sadie came back,
picked up the ball, and threw it
so hard no one could catch it.
Uh-oh.
It went crashing
through the kitchen window.
They went inside—what a mess!
Bits of broken glass all over,
including on the cake.

Mama said they couldn't eat it.
  That's when Sadie started crying
    and everyone went home.

Molly and Mama both tried
  to talk to Henry and explain
    what had happened. He kept asking,
What did I say wrong?
  They answered, *Nothing.*
    Henry, it is not your fault.
But they couldn't fix the birthday cake,
  the broken window,
    or the ruined birthday.

After that, Henry decided:
  He would only talk at home,
    to Mama and Papa,
and, of course, to Molly.

7. SCHOOL
AUGUST 1939

The other children Henry's age were starting school.
    The principal came and showed Mama and Papa
        a picture of a hearing aid.
Maybe this would help Henry
    hear his teacher, he said.
        It was big and heavy and expensive.
Papa had barely started his new job—
    they could never save enough to buy one.
        Molly listened carefully
when Mama asked what he meant by
maybe. Even if they could afford it,
        no one could promise it would help.

After the principal left, Molly asked,
    What does alternative *mean?*
        and Papa said, *There might be*
a school for deaf children
    where Henry could be taught—
        but it is in another city.
Molly asked,
    How would Henry get there every day?
        Papa's voice was gentle when he answered,
He would have to leave home
    and go to live there. We'd only see him
        once a year, at Christmas.

Molly looked at Henry, playing with his
    rock collection in a corner of the kitchen.
        No! she said. *No. No. No.*
Even as she repeated it,
    she knew—
        she and Henry
would not be the ones
    to say
        what happened next.

She didn't know
    the school for deaf children
        could say no to Henry.

THE MEN WITH KEYS
RIVERVIEW, 1939

the tall skinny one
    (Henry thinks of him as "Slim Jim")
the one who doesn't have much hair
    ("Baldy")
the one with burn scars on his face and neck
    ("Appleman," because one scar looks like an apple)
the one who comes in every morning and blows his whistle,
    then jerks back Henry's blanket
    when the whistle doesn't wake him up
    ("Blanket Man")
the one who looks like an angry barking dog
    and kicks the kids who don't jump up to obey,
    including Henry when he doesn't see him coming

Henry watches out for that one
    ("Barker").
        He looks at what the other kids are doing,
            and does it.
            Fast.

THE BOYS ON THE WARD

Thirty-three boys in gray-green clothes:
One bangs his head against the wall.
Another lets the flies land on his face.
One boy sees that Henry doesn't hear
    and taps him on the shoulder
      to warn him if he might get kicked.
Henry sticks close to that boy.
    He watches people's mouths
    when they say the boy's name
    and guesses that they're saying
        Ted.
One of Ted's legs
    is shorter than the other.
One arm
    hangs loose at his side.
With his other arm
    he motions: *Follow me.*
    Do what I do.
So Henry does.

HENRY, WATCHING

From his bed at the far end of the ward,
Henry sees a mouse run under
seven beds, across the floor,
and back into the wall. He points it out
to Ted, who tilts his head to one side,
thinking. Henry pretends to catch
the mouse and hold it in his hands.
Ted points to Barker's jacket, hanging
on a hook, and shows Henry his idea:
If we catch the mouse, we should put it
in his pocket. They laugh together.
Even though Henry knows they'll never
really catch the mouse, it still
makes him smile to imagine Barker's face
    when the mouse
        jumps out.

TEAMWORK

A little boy with curly hair comes
onto the ward.
    Where did this boy come from? Henry wonders.
        He has seen a group of little children playing outdoors.
    Why is he here?
        Maybe when those little boys get big enough
        they come to live with us.
    Where did he get that picture postcard he carries everywhere?
Henry thinks they call him Billy. He can tell
Billy is scared. He remembers how he felt
when he first arrived, how glad he was
when Ted was nice to him.

Then Henry sees a big boy take Billy's
postcard and start acting like it belongs
to him. He's not sure if Billy understands
that it's been stolen—there are a lot of things
Billy doesn't seem to understand. But Henry
knows for sure, it isn't fair to steal from someone
just because he's small and might not notice.

Henry hasn't figured out the big boy's name,
but he decides to call him James. He watches
James hide the postcard at the bottom

of the cabinet beside his own bed.
Henry nudges Ted, and they
start watching for a chance
to get Billy's postcard back.

Ted touches a finger to his forehead
to say, *I have an idea.* He points to Henry,
then points to where James hid the postcard.
Henry thinks he means,
    You go get the postcard.
Henry shakes his head, pretends
to hold up a set of keys, points to Barker,
then to James. Ted seems to understand
what Henry means: Barker and James
are bigger than he and Henry are.
Ted holds up one finger:
    Wait a minute.

They watch and wait. When the men with keys
are busy, Ted walks over to the little hole
where the mouse ran into the wall,
and he starts jumping up and down,
waving his arm and pointing.
The men and boys run over to see
why Ted is so excited.

There isn't really any mouse; it's just a trick.
While everyone is distracted, Henry quickly
gets the postcard back. It's easy—open

James's cabinet, grab the postcard,
hide it under his own shirt, and then run over
to the crowd around the mouse hole
and pretend he's been there the whole time.

It only takes a minute.
After everyone goes back to whatever
they were doing before, Henry gives
the postcard back to Billy, who looks up
at Henry with a happy smile.
Ted and Henry look around to be sure
no one is watching; then they lift the edge
of Billy's mattress and show him
how to hide the postcard underneath.

Henry and Ted keep an eye on James.
They don't look directly at him,
but they see when he discovers
that the postcard is missing,
see him glance across the room
at Billy, as if he's thinking: *Maybe that kid
is smarter than I thought.* Ted and Henry
smile at each other. James looks at
Ted, and then at several other boys,
one at a time, sizing them up.

But he looks straight past Henry, as if
    he isn't even there.

WATCH OUT, HENRY

Do people think
if they don't hear me talk,
that means I don't have
thoughts?

Henry considers this, realizes
he could hide inside
the person people think he is.
It's tempting—
he could get away with anything.
He'd be almost invisible.

Then he hears Molly's voice,
clear and strong, as if
she's right there in the room with him:
    Watch out, Henry—
    what if you pretend to be that person
    and then you accidentally turn into him?

HENRY'S WINDOW

Henry can sit on his bed and look
out through the room's only window—
dirty glass with a spiderweb
in one of the top corners.
Sometimes Henry watches
the spider catch a fly and eat it.
One afternoon it catches two flies
and eats one.
    Maybe, Henry thinks, *it will save*
    the other one, just in case
    it doesn't catch a fly tomorrow.
Henry names the spider Rex.

An old oak tree scratches the tip
of one branch against the window.
Just below that branch, another
holds a messy nest. Henry likes to watch
the squirrels that live there—four small ones,
two big—as they scamper up and down the tree.

At night, he lies in bed and looks out
through the branches,
sees how they hold the moon

as it grows round.
  Night after night,
  it fades away to nothing,
  then comes back,
  just like it does at home.

    What is Molly doing right now?
    Is Papa still working or did he lose his job again?
    When will Mama come back to get me?

BEYOND THE TREES, A FENCE

From his window,
Henry looks down at his new world.
Just below this building, a row of trees
lines the edge of a grassy field.
Beyond the trees,
a fence with a closed gate.

> *Is that gate locked?*
> *Could a boy squeeze through*
> *the little space beside it?*

Beyond the fence, the road.

> *I wonder what's inside that barn we passed*
> *the day we came here on the bus.*

Beyond the road, a river.

> *If I got on a boat, where would the river take me?*

Most afternoons, a bus goes by,
like the one he and Mama rode to come here,
that same gray dog painted on its side.
It looks like it's running fast.

> *I wish I could run as fast as that dog.*

Sometimes the bus slows down,
then stops,
so people can get off.

Henry waits and watches by the window.
  One of these days, Mama will get off
  that bus, and come and get me.

Mornings, it goes by the other way.
People wait beside the road,
and when the bus stops, they get on.
He remembers: *Mama gave our tickets to the driver.*
  If I had a ticket, could I
  get on and ride the bus back home?
  How do you get a ticket?
  They probably cost money.
  How do you get money?

A FIELD OF GRASS, A PATH

Between the tree outside his window
and the fence, a field of grass,
a path across it.

Henry and twenty other boys
walk along the path
three times each day,
from this building, where they sleep,
to that one, where they eat.
They're supposed to walk
in pairs, and Henry walks with Ted.
Billy came after the others were paired up,
and didn't have a partner,
so Henry took him by the hand, and Ted said,
    Come on, Billy, walk with us.
Henry likes these walks outside.
He wonders,
    What about the four boys
    who can't get to the meal place
    because their wheelchairs
    won't go down the stairs?

    What about the three held tight
    by blankets that keep them in their beds

all day and night?

Or the two
who have to wear those shirts
with the two sleeves tied together
so the boys can't use their hands?

And the four strapped into chairs
in the long dark hallway?

Henry never sees any of those boys eating,
but he knows they have to, somehow.

Someone, he thinks, *must bring them food*
while the rest of us are walking
to the meal place.

BLANKET MAN

Some mornings, Henry is awake
  when all the other boys
  jump out of bed at the same time.
He sees Blanket Man blow a whistle
  and yell—probably something like,
  Everybody up!
He remembers how Papa's clock
  rang an alarm bell every morning,
  so he could get to work on time.

But usually Henry is still fast asleep
  when Blanket Man jerks back his blanket
  to yank him into morning.

Ted's bed is across from Henry's. He sees
  what happens, and it's obvious
  that Henry doesn't like it. Who would?
  He tries to help by gently shaking
  Henry's shoulder. Henry sees him say
  something to Blanket Man. Maybe it's
  See, here's how to wake up my friend.

It doesn't work.
The next time Blanket Man jerks Henry's blanket back,
  he looks across at Ted and laughs.

Ted and Henry hate that man.
    If only a nice one, such as Baldy,
    would be there in the mornings.
But Baldy only comes in the afternoons.
    Henry keeps thinking
    until he finally gets a good idea.
He can't explain it without talking,
    so he decides to speak to Ted.
    I know what we can do, he says.
Ted says something, and Henry guesses
    it's *What? You can talk?*
    He says, *I can talk, but I can't hear.*
Ted looks like he's thinking about that,
    so Henry adds, *Don't tell. Some people*
    get mad if I say something wrong.
Ted nods, points to Henry's head, meaning,
    Okay. What's your idea?
    Henry hopes he can explain it.
We need a string, he says, and goes on
    to explain the whole idea, smiling
    when Ted understands. That afternoon,
Ted talks to Baldy, and the next day,
    Baldy brings a ball of string and helps them
    measure and cut it to the right length.
That night they tie it
    between Ted's bed
    and Henry's ankle.

Their idea works! In the morning, Blanket Man
    looks long and hard at Ted and Henry,
    sitting up in their beds, grinning.
Blanket Man looks like he knows
    he's been outsmarted
    and he doesn't like it.

THE PATH CURVES AROUND

When he's walking to the meal place,
Henry counts eight other buildings
made of dark red brick, like his.

Where the path curves around
behind his building, people walk in lines
from one building to another.

Some of the people in the other lines
are girls. Some are men. Some
are grown-up women like his mother,
only not as pretty.

The men wear gray-green clothes,
the same color as the boys'.
The girls' and women's clothes are a color
he can't name—maybe their clothes were pink,
or even red, a long time ago, but now
they're brownish-gray.

Two extra people always walk
with the people in the lines—
two men with the boys,
two women with the girls.

One at the front of the line,
the other at the back.

Those men and women wear
dark blue clothes.
Some of the women wear
white caps and aprons.

Henry is sure those men
and women all have keys.

INSIDE THE FENCE, SOMETHING

Across the road, inside a chain-link fence,
something Henry doesn't understand:
pathways wind through it, like the place
he went one time with Molly and his parents
and the pastor when their friend
Mrs. Grayson died.

He remembers the prayer they said
and the song they sang together.
But this place can't be a cemetery:
no monuments, no gravestones.
Only tall grass and weeds and
rows of little sticks—what are they?

KICKBALL

Henry looks out the window at the grassy field.
   Once in a while, some boys go outdoors
      to run around and kick a ball.
         I could do that, Henry thinks.
The next time Baldy comes, when he
picks up a ball and says something,
and ten boys line up to go outside,
Henry gets in line and goes with them.
He can figure out this game:
Baldy rolls the ball to one boy,
who kicks it and sends it flying.
Then that boy runs around in a circle
while others chase the ball.
It looks like you're supposed to touch
three rocks along the way.

When it's Ted's turn, it's hard for him
to catch or kick the ball, but he keeps trying.
Henry sees how he could help.
He stays close to Ted, and when the ball
comes their way, Henry catches it and sets
it down so Ted can kick it, standing
on his short leg, kicking with the longer one.
He starts to walk, as fast as he can,

to the first rock, but Baldy catches
the ball in the air and Ted goes back
to where Henry helped him kick it.

Then Baldy points to Henry:
Your turn. So Henry stands
where Ted was, and Baldy rolls
the ball to him. Henry kicks it hard
      and it soars
            across the grass,
                  over the fence.
James chases the ball, and Henry sees—
right there where the fence meets the trees,
      there *is* a space a boy can fit through.

Henry's not sure if he's supposed to wait
for James to get back to where they're playing.
The other boys are waving their arms
and yelling—Henry guesses
they must be saying:
      Run, Henry, run!
And Ted is pointing to the first rock,
so Henry runs to it, and keeps going
until he gets all the way back
to where he kicked the ball.
That seems to make people happy.
Henry is happy too.

He understands the game—
kick and run and touch the rocks
until you get back where you started.
There might be some other rules,
but no one seems to care
too much about them. Kick and run,
and help Ted if he needs it.
Henry can do this.
He likes the outdoor time.
It's easier to breathe out here.
He wishes they could go out every day,
but Baldy is the only one who lets them.

As they walk back inside,
   Henry tucks away what he has learned today:
      There is a boy-sized space
      between the trees and fence.

WHERE IS JAMES?

OCTOBER 1939

Henry doesn't think James knows
who took the postcard back
and helped Billy hide it.
He hasn't seen James do anything else
that mean or sneaky, but still
he keeps an eye on him.
You never know.

Then one morning, Blanket Man
thinks James isn't moving
fast enough—he pushes him
into the breakfast line, grabs him
by the shoulders, shoves him out the door.
James shoves back, not very hard,
but hard enough for Blanket Man to punish
him by making him miss breakfast.
He has to sit there, watching all the other boys
eat toast and oatmeal, without getting
a single bite himself. Henry knows that is
not right. He's never talked to James
and doesn't want to start now,
but he wants him to know
he saw what happened.
He gives him a piece of toast

when no one's looking. James is surprised,
and Henry knows he says, *Thanks,*
as he hides the toast under his shirt.

James still looks mad
when they line up to go back,
and Henry sees him slip out of the line.
He nudges Ted and they watch James
run and hide behind a tree.
When they get back to the ward,
they look out the window and see
him running from one tree
to the next, staying in the shadows.
Then he squeezes past the fence
and keeps on running until they
can't see him anymore.
    Henry asks Ted, *Should we tell?*
    Ted shakes his head. *No.*
Henry doesn't know where James is going.
He hopes the men with keys won't catch him.

SEARCHING UNDER BEDS

When the boys line up for lunch
and the attendants count them,
Blanket Man and Barker know
someone is missing. Who?
They make all the boys
go stand beside their beds.
    James.
Where is he? Within minutes,
four other men with keys are on the ward,
searching under beds, inside every cabinet,
pulling dirty sheets out of the laundry bin.

They don't find James.

When the other boys finally get to lunch,
the food is cold (fried eggs that look like rubber),
and a fly has landed in the milk.

Henry hopes James has a home to run to.
If he gets there, maybe his family
won't make him come back here.

THAT NIGHT

Mama. Papa. Molly.
As Henry falls asleep that night.
he sees their faces shining
in the sunlight of the kitchen.
In the morning, he's still dreaming
that he's walking down the road
from his house to Mrs. Grayson's.
She smiles at him, gives him
a cup of hot chocolate and a cookie.
He doesn't want to wake up, but he
feels the string tug at his ankle.

And here he is again.

NOT FAIR

In the morning, Blanket Man and Barker
and two other men with keys
bring James back to the ward.
He's limping in a way he wasn't yesterday.
His face is bruised; one eye is swollen shut.

They make sure the other boys
get a good look at James before they
take him to the hallway where the chairs
have straps, put him in a chair,
and pull the buckles tight. Henry didn't even
like James very much,
but he knows for sure
this is not fair.

HENRY COUNTS THE DAYS

NOVEMBER 1939

Henry goes out to the hallway every day
to let James know he sees him there.
Some days Billy follows him, and Ted
went with him once, but it seemed to
make Ted mad, so most days it's only Henry.
He counts the days—five . . . eight . . . fifteen . . .
twenty-five . . . He hopes it won't get past one hundred,
because that's as high as he can count.
On day twenty-eight, Barker glances at Henry and Billy
standing beside James, watching in silence.
After he has tightened James's straps,
Barker looks at James and says something
that looks to Henry like a threat.
Barker waits for James to nod agreement,
and then he loosens all the straps.
Henry wonders,
> *Will James get up and kick him,*
> *and then run away again?*
He hopes so; he thinks that's what he would do.
But he understands why James stands up
and then just walks away
without saying or doing anything.

WE MISS YOU

CHRISTMAS 1939

It gets colder.
Henry wishes he could find out
how long he has to stay here.
Sometimes the men with keys
bring letters for the boys,
and one day, they give one to him.
He sees an *H* on the envelope,
    like the ones Molly showed him
        on the presents. *H* means Henry!
He tears the letter open and there's
    a picture inside. He knows Molly drew it:
        a table with a pie on it, four chairs around it,
three people and one empty chair.
    In a corner of the picture,
        a Christmas tree with a silver star on top.
This is his sister's way of telling him,
    It's Christmas, Henry,
        and we miss you.
He wishes he had paper and a pencil
and an envelope like that
and someone who would help him
send a picture back to her.

At first, the letter makes him happy,

but that night Henry dreams
of home again, and when he wakes up
at Riverview, and it smells the same
as always, Henry can't stop tears
from trickling into his ears.

HE'S SEVEN NOW

JULY 1940

The days are hot, like they were
when Henry first came to Riverview.
He gets another letter, with a picture
    of a birthday cake. He counts the candles,
        so he knows he's seven now.
He tries to push the thought away,
but it keeps returning:
    What if Mama never comes to get me?
    Papa?
    Wouldn't Molly tell them not to leave me here?

Every so often new boys come,
and he never sees them leave.
Sometimes the big boys leave. At first,
Henry thinks they get to go home.
But then one day James leaves, and the next day
Henry sees him walking in a line outside
with other big boys.
    He didn't go home.
    He only moved to a different building.

A SMALL BROWN BIRD

SEPTEMBER 1940

The pail under the dripping ceiling
    fills up fast today. Drip. Drip. Drip.
    Henry keeps an eye on it, and, carefully,
    before it overflows, he carries it
        between the rows of twenty beds,
        over to the sink. Billy follows him
        and helps by wiping up the little puddles
        on the floor. Then they go together
        to set the pail back where it was.
    When it fills again,
    Henry empties it again. Four times a day
    if it's raining hard like this.
He doesn't know why he's the only one
    who seems to notice when the pail is full,
    but since he is, he empties it, with Billy
    like his little shadow, helping.

Afternoons, he watches
    at the window: he likes to watch
        the small brown birds that come—
        landing, flying off, returning
        to a patch of grass beneath the oak tree,
        where they sway back and forth
        as they eat the little weed-seeds

left over from the flowers
on their sturdy stalks.

Peck. Peck. Peck.

But not today. When it rains
like this, the birds
don't come so much.

THE WINDOW

That crack in the windowpane
    didn't used to be there. One evening,
    Billy started crying
    and he wouldn't stop.
Ted and Henry couldn't figure out
    why he was crying, and Barker,
    the only grown-up on the ward,
    was ignoring him.
Ted put his hands over his ears
    and said something to Billy—that's how
    Henry knew the sound of crying bothered Ted,
    but Billy kept it up. No one could stop him.
After it went on a while, Barker threw a shoe
    across the room
    that missed Billy and cracked
    the window. Henry remembered
a long time ago at home, when bits of
    broken glass got on his birthday cake
    and Sadie cried. At least this window
    didn't shatter like that one did.

Now, sometimes, Henry looks at that crack
    and wonders:
        If the shoe had hit my friend,
        would he be cracked like this?

THAT ROOM

Henry remembers the steps, the door
where he once entered. Is that room
still there? The one with big soft chairs.

A carpet on the floor.
The room that smelled like
wilting summer flowers.

No one in that room
wore faded gray-green clothes.
Some people there smelled clean.

MAMA AND A GIRL

MARCH 1941

The weather changes—instead of rain,
there's snow now. It looks fresh and nice,
but Henry's hands and feet are always cold.

His days all start the same way: get out of bed,
put on his day clothes and a jacket, walk over
to the breakfast place to eat toast and oatmeal.

And then, one surprising day, Appleman
comes with clean clothes, brown and white,
and a pair of shoes not as worn out
as the ones Henry usually wears, the ones
with cardboard shoved inside to cover up
the holes worn through the soles.
Henry puts the clothes on—
they almost fit. He can squeeze
his feet into the shoes.

Appleman leads Henry
down the hallway he remembers
from the day he first arrived.

The heavy door opens, closes behind him.
Appleman leaves him there.

And there she is:
   Mama,
      and a girl
who looks like Molly, only bigger.
   The girl smiles, reaches out
      for Henry's hand, and then he sees:
it *is* Molly. He remembers
   how her name sounds
      from long ago, when he could hear.
His mouth opens, and he says it: *Molly!*
   and then he sees her mouth say, *Henry.*
      His name.
And Henry figures out
   that he
      is bigger too.

NEW SOCKS

Mama gives Henry a peppermint,
    an orange, and two new pairs of socks.
        He takes off the shoes—his feet are rough;
his jagged toenails snag a thread on his new sock.
    But once he gets the socks on, he smiles big.
        He almost feels like he's back home.

Mama straightens out the socks, then looks into
    Henry's eyes and starts to talk, saying every word
        slowly, hoping Henry understands:

We would have come before,
    but we have no extra money.
        I've been saving for this trip, taking in
mending from the neighbors,
    selling eggs when the hens are laying.
        But times are hard, my darling. I'm so sorry.

Henry thinks she says *money* and *bending*,
    maybe *eggs*. He doesn't know she says *sorry*,
        but he understands that she still loves him.
Henry keeps on smiling. When he turns to Molly,
    she doesn't try to talk. She makes her hand
        into a wolf, like she used to in the dark,

when the lamplight cast shadows
    on their wall at home. Henry thinks
        for a minute before his hand makes
the rabbit, and hops away from Molly's wolf.
    He lets her catch it like they always did.
        He wonders if his sister will still
pull him close—she does—but she does not
    try to kiss his hair. It's been so long,
        and they have both grown taller.

GOODBYE

Henry is happy, thinking, *Finally,*
    they've come to get me out of here.
        We'll all go home together,
        and Papa will be there.
It's been a long time since he's talked out loud
    to anyone except Ted, and he only talks to Ted
        when no one else can hear him.
        But he finds the words he needs.
Let's go home now. I want to see Papa.
    He can see that Molly and Mama are pleased
        that he is talking. He knows
        they understand him.
But something else—a worried look—flashes
    between the two of them. Henry can't quite
        tell what it means. He knows
        he doesn't like it.
Then Appleman comes back, and it looks to Henry
    like he plans to take him back to the ward.
        The smile leaves Henry's face.
        His eyes go dark.
Appleman motions toward the door,
    and Henry sees for sure: He is not going home.
        He turns to look at Molly and his mother,
        sees Molly wave her hand at him.

Goodbye, Henry.

Henry hollers: *Take me home!*

Appleman says, *What?*

jerks Henry by the arm, pushes him

back through the heavy door. Molly jumps up

as the door closes behind Henry. She runs over,

hears the lock click shut. It cuts off

Mama's promise:

We'll come again at Christmas.

She doesn't hear, behind the door,

how Appleman sneers: *You little sneak.*

Pretending you can't talk.

Trying to make us think you're deaf.

THE HEAVY DOOR

Molly jams her fists into her pockets.
    That man didn't have to be like that.
        Henry would have gone back through
the heavy door if the attendant had been gentle.
    Why did he say *What?* like that, as if
        it was the first time he'd heard Henry speak?
Does Henry talk to anyone in this awful place?
    Mama holds her tears until they're back outside
        and the Greyhound bus is coming down the road.

REMEMBERING AUGUST 1939
A CHILD LIKE THIS

On the long bus ride home,
    Mama cries
        and blows her nose into her hankie.

Molly wishes they could go back to the first time
    those ladies came. Mama scrubbed the floor
        and Molly dusted furniture.
They washed every napkin, spread them out to dry,
    put a doily on the kitchen table
        to cover up the burn mark.
Henry picked a big bouquet
    of hollyhocks and zinnias,
        filled a jam jar halfway up with water.
He put the flowers in it, set it on the doily—
    all of them trying so hard to make the house
        look like a proper place to raise
        a child like this.

That's what the ladies
    kept calling Henry.
        A child like what? Molly wondered.
Henry, scared and quiet, hid
    behind the kitchen door,
        the ladies watching

like they hoped to catch him
　　doing something wrong.
　　　　We will help you decide, they said,
　　　　where the boy is best suited.
They must have seen the question
　　on Mama's face, so they made it clear:
　　　　the State School for the Deaf
　　　　or
　　　　Riverview Home for the Feebleminded.
Mama gasped.
　　The School for the Deaf,
　　　　of course! she said.
We will see, said the ladies,
　　and they gave her a card
　　　　with the school's address,
　　　　and told her to take Henry there
　　　　for testing.

AWAY FROM ALL HE KNEW

Molly remembers Henry looked so scared
    when he and Mama got on the bus that morning,
        his first time going so far away
from all he knew at home.

Mama took him to the School for the Deaf.
    It was dark when the bus brought them back home,
        and Molly saw a different kind of darkness
in Mama's eyes: sadness, anger, something else,
    new and hard to name. After Henry went to bed,
        Mama and Papa sat down at the table.
Molly sat down with them.
    I suppose, Mama said,
        you may as well hear this.

    They didn't even show us around the school,
    she began. *We never saw a single class or met*
    any of the students or teachers. They took
    Henry into a little room and gave him
    what they called a simple test.
    "Can he be taught," they asked,
    "to blow out a candle?"

Molly knew that would be easy for Henry.
He blew out his birthday candles
every year. He loved that.

But Mama went on:
He was frightened.
He didn't understand.
She described the candle on a table,
how the testing man would light it,
blow it out, light it again, and point to Henry.
Now you do it was what he meant.
Henry pushed his chair back.
The man lit the candle.
Blew it out.
Again and again—ten times.
And Henry wouldn't do it.
The man kept writing in his notebook.
Henry got more and more upset.
When he crawled under the table
and refused to come back out,
the man said, *I'm sorry, ma'am.*
Your son appears to be
unteachable.

It took Molly a few minutes
to understand what all this meant.

Didn't you tell them, she demanded,
how Henry used to hum along
to the songs Mr. Grayson played on his harmonica?
Or how, when he was only three years old,
before he got that earache,
Henry could hear a story once,
and tell it back to anyone who'd listen?
He can count up to a hundred!
He can find birds' nests and catch frogs.

Mama closed her eyes before she answered,
You know that.
Papa and I know.
Henry is smart.
But he can be shy. He can be stubborn.
Today he was both at the same time.
That was all the man saw.
He wouldn't listen to me.
He acted like he knew more about our Henry
from that one silly test
than anyone, including
Henry's own mother,
could ever know.

She paused.
Those two ladies will be back next week
to tell us their decision.

And then when they came back
and Molly heard their words—
Riverview
and *Feebleminded*—
she just stood there
with her fists in her pockets
and her mouth clamped shut
as if she
had forgotten
how to talk.

She never told them how Henry saved her life
that time, when a raccoon got underneath
the porch, and Molly tried to coax it out.
Even though he was three and she was eight,
Henry was the one who said, *It might have rabies.*
So they left it alone and told Papa,
and he trapped it, and took it to a place
where they said Henry was right.
Molly wishes she had told those ladies,
I might have died if Henry
had not been so smart that day.

When the ladies came with their decision,
one said,
He will be better off.
And then the other added,

Surely you understand,
you cannot care for a child like this
at home.
The first, again:
You must think about your entire family,
not only this one boy.
She looked at Molly when she said that.
And Molly
did not say a single word
to defend herself or Henry.
Later, she thought of what she might have said:
You leave Henry here, where he belongs.
I'll teach him how to read and write and do arithmetic.
I don't care about the teasing—
those big boys' words
don't mean a thing.

But the words
started singing in her head that day:
They'll take your brother to the loony bin,
loony bin, loony bin.
They'll take him to the loony bin,
and they should take you, too.

When the kids at school sang that song—
first two, then three, then six of them—
Molly stuck out her chin and answered:

Sticks and stones will break my bones
but words can never hurt me.

It wasn't true—their words
    cut deep-down into her,
        and maybe into Henry, too,
even though he didn't hear them, only saw
    how those kids' faces were like
        snarled-up bramble bushes.
Could he tell by looking at them
    that their mouths
        were full of thorns?

That awful day, those dressed-up ladies just kept talking,
    never asking Mama what she thought
        would be best for Henry.
And the whole time,
    Molly stood there saying
        nothing.

Papa was working on a farm ten miles away.
    When he got home two days later, Mama repeated
        the ladies' words, and Papa answered
every argument:
    We have been caring for Henry at home all his life.
    It will be hard for Molly if he goes away.
Then Mama got to the one that Molly knew
    could not possibly be true:

He will be happier with those of his own kind.
When she heard that, Molly finally argued back:
   We are his own kind!
      Papa was quiet for a minute before he said,
That is true.
   And then he added, as gently as he could,
      The kind that doesn't get to make the rules.
Mama and Papa studied the paper
   the ladies left behind, full of big words,
      and hard to read. After a long time, Papa said,
It doesn't sound like we have much of a choice.
   Molly saw Mama's tears fall on the paper
   as she and Papa signed it.

HENRY'S EMPTY CHAIR
NOVEMBER 1941

We've saved enough money for two Greyhound tickets,
  Papa says to Molly. *And we've decided—for Henry's*
    Christmas visit, I will go with Mama.

Mama knits a sweater,
  two pairs of mittens,
    and a stocking cap.
Molly helps her make a fruitcake.
  Papa decides that he will buy
    a sack of peppermints.

Molly draws more pictures
  for them to take to Riverview:
    Snowball's three new kittens,
the bonfire they had on Halloween,
  and another picture of their table
    with Henry's empty chair.

PEARL HARBOR
DECEMBER 1941

Seventeen days before their trip to Riverview, the news:

   Pearl Harbor has been bombed.

      America is at war.

WHAT IS GOING ON?

DECEMBER 1941

Something changes at Riverview,
but Henry can't tell what has happened.
The attendants close the curtains before
they turn on any lights. Men
who used to fix the things that broke
stop coming: When the doorknob
falls off, it stays off. A sink clogs up
and water overflows. A toilet, too.

The attendants, and the boys like Ted and Henry
who can help, work harder, but mostly, things
at Riverview just don't get fixed.

Slim Jim and Barker lean over a newspaper
looking worried.
 What is going on? Henry wonders.
The paper is discarded on the ward,
and Ted and Henry study it: pictures of explosions,
boats, men trying to swim away from fire.
A gray-haired man. Giant letters.
Henry points to something on the paper,
  and tells Ted:
 That's an H, like my name, Henry.
They wish they could read the words
and piece everything together.

AT HOME, THEY TRY TO SING

The war changes everything.
    Papa learns to be a welder and works all day,
        through supper until midnight, seven days a week.

Mama starts working at the bakery when the man
    who had that job leaves to join the army. Molly
        tries to help by doing things Mama used to do.

The money is still there—maybe they'll even buy another ticket,
    so Molly can go too—but now they can't get enough
        time off from work for the trip to visit Henry.

On Christmas Eve, Papa lights the candles
    and they try to sing:
        Holy infant, so tender and mild . . .
Mama sings that much, but then
    her voice breaks into pieces,
        so they stop.
Papa holds her in his arms
    to comfort her.
        I promised, she keeps saying.

The thought crosses Molly's mind:
    Henry didn't hear the promise.
        Even though she doesn't say it

right out loud,
    just thinking it
        makes her ashamed.

LUCKY

Molly knows that she's the lucky one.
    She does.
Mama and Papa never actually
    say this,
but she knows they think,
    It might
have been the other way around.
    You could
be at Riverview, Henry here
    at home.

So don't complain.

Molly does not
    complain
when Mama knits those socks
    and mittens,
plus two hats and a sweater—
    for Henry.
She doesn't say a word when
    Mama uses
up the yarn. Molly knows yarn
    is expensive.

She doesn't say she needs a new
    warm hat
herself, and although
    the sleeves
of her only sweater no longer reach
    her wrists,
she truly does want Henry
    to have
whatever they can give him—
    because
there is so much
    they can't.

Henry is the constant undercurrent
    of their lives.
Even when they can't go see him,
    whether or not
they talk about him, Henry
    is the glue
that holds their family
    together.

At home, Henry's absence is
    ever-present.
At school, Molly never
    mentions him.

AN ORANGE

One bright snowy day, the attendants
put shoes and nice clothes
on three boys, take them out,
bring them back. They return
to the cold room with gifts—
Henry thinks they must be from
their mothers.

> *Where is my mother?*
> *Where are Molly and Papa?*
> *When they come, they might bring*
> *new socks again. I want to give them*
> *something too. Would Molly*
> *like the blue feather I found*
> *one day last summer? And the small*
> *striped stone—Mama might like that.*

Baldy comes for Ted, gives him
clean clothes, leads him away—
to the nice room, Henry guesses.

When Ted comes back, he holds
an orange in his hand. He peels it
and gives half to Henry,
who gives half of his half to Billy.

Maybe this is Christmas.
Henry hopes
his mother and his sister
will come to see him soon.
Maybe Papa will come too.
If they bring him an orange,
he'll share it with Ted and Billy.

But no one comes
to visit Henry.

SHE LETS HER FRIENDS FORGET

Molly goes to a New Year's Eve party,
 and all her friends are talking
  about brothers who enlisted, fathers
who might get called up. Molly says,
 My father learned to be a welder.
 That's important war work.
The conversation is about to
 flow right past her, when a girl
  whose brother has been drafted says,

Molly, you're lucky
 you don't have
  a brother.

Molly knows what this girl means:
 an older brother. One who would
  have to go to war. And yes, again,
Molly knows *she's lucky.*
 But she has been friends with this girl
  since before first grade. The girl knew Henry
before he went to Riverview. Everyone did!
 But no one, among all the chatter, corrects her.
  Not a single person says,
  Molly has a brother—his name is Henry.

And Molly doesn't speak his name herself.
  She lets her friends forget
    that she ever had a brother.

HENRY HOLDS THE DUSTPAN

FEBRUARY 1942

The men with keys start leaving.
Just when Henry thinks he's figured out
who he might trust a little bit,
that man is gone, and someone else
comes in to take his place,
with quirks and habits of his own.
There's one who thinks it's funny
to turn the shower cold, then hot, then
cold again, making Henry and the others
do a kind of dance. Henry tries
to ignore it and clean himself the best
he can, so the smells he can't help
breathing in come from
the rooms around him,
but not from his own skin.

Then one day, Shower-Dance Man leaves
and never comes again, but
this time, no one takes his place.
Soon after that, Appleman is gone,
and then two more men leave. Where once
there were nine men with keys, now it's only
Baldy, Barker, Blanket Man, and Slim Jim.

Henry has known the rhythm of his days,
marked off by breakfast, lunch, dinner
in the meal place, something hot to drink
with a small snack before they go to bed.

Most days now, they only have two meals.
Some days only one.
No snacks. No hot drinks.
The food is always cold.

The boys keep doing their work.
Henry and Ted stack the dirty plates.
Henry and Billy carry them back to the kitchen.
The three of them wipe down the tables.
Ted holds the broom in his good arm
and sweeps the floor. Henry holds
the dustpan. Or they switch off—
Henry sweeps; Ted holds the dustpan.
They like doing those chores together.

SPILLED TOMATO SOUP

MARCH 1942

Ted and Henry and Billy. Billy, Henry, and Ted.
It's good to have friends to sit with
when you're eating. Billy watches
Ted and Henry, helps them clear the tables,
wipe them down, then sweep the floor. If Billy
makes mistakes, Ted and Henry fix them.

And then one snowy day in March—
it happens fast—Billy drops
a not-quite-empty crock of soup.
He runs to Henry, taps him on the shoulder,
points to the mess—Henry will know
what to do. And Billy's right: Henry
quickly steps in, shows Billy and the other kids
how to step around the mess. Then he goes
to get a broom and sees that Ted
already has one, and is on his way to help.

Ted hesitates—he tries to sweep up the broken
pieces of the crock, but it's hard to do that
without smearing spilled tomato soup across the floor.

That's when Barker strides across the room, sees Billy
standing there beside the mess, grabs the arm
he raises to defend himself, twists it behind
Billy's back, and slaps him. Slaps him again.

Ted moves fast, swings his broom at Barker,
and the broom has soup on it,
    which gets on Barker's clothes
    and looks a little bit like blood.
    (But isn't.)

Forget about Billy—Barker lets him go,
swings at Ted. Henry puts a hand on Billy's
shoulder, and they stand there watching
as Barker pulls a lever, and two more
men rush in and tackle Ted. They lift him up,
strap him into a chair.
    Oh no, Henry thinks,
    the rows of chairs along the hallway!

After that, each morning Ted is strapped
down. He has to stay like that all day.

At first, he fights it. Kicks the wall.
Rocks his chair so hard it tips on its side.
Pounds the fist of his good arm on the floor
until someone comes to stop him.
Once, he tries to bite Slim Jim.

And then one day, Ted just sits there.
Henry sees the light in his friend's eyes grow dim.
He sits beside Ted
on the cold and dirty floor and tries
to think of ways to make him smile.

He finds a scrap of paper and a pencil, draws
a picture: Barker with a mouse in his hair.
Henry draws keys in his hand,
and then erases them, and draws
three boys—one with curly hair,
a little smaller than the other two.
    The boys have keys.
    And they are running.

HOW TO HIDE THE BUCKLES

A new attendant comes. Henry watches
Barker show him who to strap to chairs,
and how to hide the buckles
so that the boys can't loosen them.

How to move the boys from chairs
to beds, and tuck the blankets in around them
so tight they can't get out.

Henry counts: most boys are strapped down
for ten or twenty days. But Ted has been
out in this hallway for eighty-seven days! Why
do they keep doing this to him?

Henry looks at Ted and wonders:
Could I unbuckle my friend's straps?
If I did, would they strap me down too?
Someday we will walk right out of here,
push through that space in the fence,
and find our way back home. Where
do these attendants go when they leave
this place and don't come back?

What happens to their keys
if no one comes to take their place?

ONE PROBLEM SOLVED

JUNE 1942

There's a problem in the mornings.
The string trick doesn't work because
Ted is tucked into his bed so tight he can't
pull the string to wake up Henry.

Henry can't make Billy understand
how it's supposed to work. Usually,
Henry wakes up when light
comes in the window. Most days,
he gets up on his own before
Blanket Man jerks back his blanket.

But not always.

One morning,
Henry opens his eyes and looks around.
 Good, he thinks,
 Blanket Man has not come in yet.
And then something funny happens:

Henry farts.

A big smelly one,
worse than all the other smells at Riverview.

He could lift the edge of his blanket
and let it out a little at a time—maybe
no one would even notice.

But Henry gets a great idea:
He pulls his blanket up around his neck
and holds it tight, waiting for Blanket Man
to blow his whistle and wake up
the other boys. Henry pretends
he's still asleep, and Blanket Man
does what he always does.

Ha!

Blanket Man jumps back and waves his arms
as if Henry's bed has caught on fire.
It looks to Henry like he's hollering,
    maybe even cussing.

The other boys start laughing,
and when Blanket Man's not looking,
Henry laughs too, jumps up,
and takes a little bow,
so everyone but Blanket Man will know
    he did that trick on purpose.

And that's the last time Blanket Man
jerks back Henry's blanket.

After that, if Henry's not awake when he comes in,
Blanket Man just taps him on the shoulder—
carefully.
And moves away.
Fast.

DOWN THE ROAD, DAYDREAMING

JULY 1942

Henry looks down from his window
at a row of sunflowers. He remembers them
from home and thinks,
It must be near my birthday. I want to go home.

When everyone returns from supper, before
it gets completely dark, one attendant leaves
and another comes. Could he catch the door
before it locks behind the man who's leaving?

Step through and stay hidden until he gets outside,
then keep close to the buildings, in the shadows
of the trees? Run to the fence, slip through
the gap? From there, it's a short walk to the road.

He remembers riding on the bus to get here—
the small towns they passed through,
and one city, where the bus stopped
and everyone got out to stretch.

Not far from here, there was
a train track with a crossing bar.
And then, *Just before we got off the bus,
we passed that rickety old barn.*

Henry can see it when he looks out the window.
He knows for sure he could run that far,
then hide and rest inside the barn. After that,
the road to his house would be long.

He'd be hungry. Tired. But if he made it—
Mama would have food when he got home.
He'd sit down at a table and have birthday cake
with his family, and go to sleep in his own bed.

He watches the river as it curves along the road,
and the birds that fly above the trees. Henry isn't
planning an escape, exactly. He is
daydreaming, to keep his mind alive.

PARENTS. SISTERS. BROTHERS. DOGS AND CATS.

Ever since Billy broke the soup crock,
and watched those three men strap Ted down,
he's been even more like Henry's shadow.

He follows him around the ward, walking
close beside him when they go to meals. Henry
doesn't mind—he pretends Billy is his brother.

Billy's bed is next to Henry's now,
and before they turn the lights out, Henry makes
the wolf with his hands, and Billy makes the rabbit.

Sometimes the rabbit gets away;
sometimes it doesn't. Either way, Billy laughs,
and Henry thinks, *Good night, my friend.*

But after the lights are out,
Henry is pretty sure that Billy
cries himself to sleep.

> *I wonder if he has a family, like I do.*
> *Did all the boys here have a home one time?*
> *Parents. Sisters. Brothers. Dogs and cats.*

PART II

CHANGE

1942–1944

THE MIDDLE BROTHER

VICTOR
NOVEMBER 1942

1.

Ninety miles from Riverview, Victor tries to sleep.
His older brother, Steven, is going off to war, and Joey,
nine, pretends he's going too. The whole town will be
gathering to celebrate the soldiers. Victor tries to keep
his thinking clear. *How can I tell my parents? I have to let
them know I'm sure of this. People can say what they will—
my conscience tells me it is never right to kill.*
I cannot turn strangers into enemies. Victor is not yet
eighteen, but soon he will be. He knows of other
men who feel as he does, and he repeats the name for
what he is: *conscientious objector.* Not: *coward.* Even
as he prepares to go to the town hall to honor his brother,
Victor knows he will have to explain: *I say no to every war.*
He gathers his courage, bundling it with love for Steven.

2.

He gathers his courage, bundling it with love for Steven,
Joey, and their parents. They've come home, and Father asks why
Victor was so quiet at the send-off. He answers: *You know my
feelings. No one can be forced to go to war. We must each be given
a chance to make that hard decision.* The four of them look
at him, waiting. Lurking in the background, the family ghost
they seldom talk about: Uncle Frank—Mother's brother—lost
in the Great War. They never say *he gave,* or *they took,*
but rather *he lost* his life. As if it might be found one day,
and maybe Father's arm beside it—that other absence of their
family life, silently lived around. Victor closes his eyes,
opens them: *I am a conscientious objector.* It feels strong to say
it, or shorten it, as he's heard others do, to *CO.* Mother asks where
Victor's clear convictions come from. Father sighs.

3.

Victor's convictions may come from Father's sighs,
from his frustrating lifelong refusal to discuss
what some have called "the war to end all wars." Just
sixteen when he joined up, now Father denies
that the loss of his right arm makes him a hero. *I might
have killed him if he hadn't shot me first, I must confess.*
He says this to Steven. And then, to Victor: *It was a mess
I couldn't get out of once I got in. The reason for that fight
was often hard to keep in mind.* Silent so long, Father tries,
now, to let both his sons know he's on their side. They
can't answer him or look at each other. They don't speak.
How can this be reconciled? If Steven lives or dies,
he will be honored by his country. Victor can't honestly say
he doesn't care if people think he's scared and weak.

4.

Let's see what he cares about. He's scared. So weak
he'd let his brother risk his life, but nope, not him.
I heard about a fellow two towns over—name was Jim—
said the same thing about his "conscience." Dirty freak!
Victor walks past his tormentors, wishing Joey had stayed
home. Joey is blazing mad—his anger mixed with shame.
Steven's been gone three weeks. Yesterday his first letter came,
and today they're mailing a reply. Victor is afraid
of what these boys will do if Joey starts yelling back.
It could easily turn into a fistfight. No: keep walking
past this group without answering their taunts. There are four
of them, likely to be more nearby. If one starts to attack,
they'll all jump in. Victor keeps an eye on Joey, talking
about anything, until they're safely back to their own door.

5.

Anything could happen before I'm back home, safe at this door,
Victor says. Aunt Muriel is visiting for three days so she can see
him off. *At least it's not prison,* she says. *What they did to me
in 1917 shouldn't happen to anyone, ever again. Sleeping on the floor
with one thin, dirty blanket . . .* She shudders, remembering the time
her own conscience called her to fight for every woman's right
to vote. She's proud of what she did, but she hopes Victor might
get out of this with fewer battle scars. It's no more of a crime
for him to refuse military service than it was for her to demonstrate
in Washington, DC. And so Victor leaves home on a late-night bus
to begin work as an attendant in a state hospital. Will it be as hard,
he wonders, as fighting fires out west? Both jobs are alternate
service for COs, but compared to war, this work won't be dangerous.
Victor gets on the bus, studying the address he's written on a card.

6.

Victor gets off the bus, studying the address written on his card.
He picks up his duffel bag and looks around. He has come to
the redbrick buildings on the edge of town. The letter said, *Go
to the main office,* so he walks across the fenced-in yard
and up a set of concrete steps. He passes boys in gray-green
clothing following a bald man along a path. They're heading for
the cafeteria, according to a broken sign on a door.
These boys seem sad. Most look at the ground. A few lean
in to look at Victor, but when he smiles, they don't smile
back. Victor finds the office—a comfortable place,
with two desks (one large, one small), a bookshelf,
filing cabinets, three folding chairs against one wall.
A man behind the large desk stands. His face
is friendly—until Victor introduces himself.

7.

Victor is friendly when he introduces himself:
I understand I've been sent because you need more
help, with so many of your attendants in the war.
The man behind the desk says, *I don't know what help*
you scrawny cowards will be. We need real men
to do this work. But I suppose if they're sending us free
labor, I'm in no position to turn it down. I can see
you're young and idealistic. Probably naïve. When
you've been here a week or two, you won't want to stay,
I promise you that. This is not as easy as you think.
Victor doesn't answer. The hard truth begins to creep
in on him: *This fellow may be right.* The man leads the way
upstairs, down a hallway, to a boys' ward. *(What's that stink?)*
Here, ninety miles from his family, he will eat and sleep.

SOMETHING IS MISSING
NOVEMBER 1942

Henry wakes up before the others—
what is different this morning?
Light, dimmed by the dusty window,
falls as usual on his blanket, but:
    Something is missing.
Henry looks around the ward
three times before his eyes come to rest
on what is wrong: Billy
is not in his bed.

SOMEONE WALKING

Henry looks out the window,
squints into the sunrise, sees
someone walking down the road—
a boy Billy's size, Billy's shape,
who walks the same way Billy walks.

It must be him. Henry thinks hard: No one
has ever come to visit Billy. He would not
know his way home—if he even has
a home. Has anyone here missed him yet?
No one else is awake. Where are the attendants?

There used to be three of them on each ward
all day. Three others were supposed to come
and stay awake at night. Now there's no one here.
Why not? Henry looks around. Someone has
left a book wedged in the door to hold it open.

Henry looks through the door, down the hallway,
into the next ward. At the far end, he sees
someone who looks like an attendant,
except he isn't wearing dark blue clothes.
His clothes are white. Who is he?

WHAT SHOULD HE DO?

First thing in the morning, someone
will come in and count the boys
as they line up for breakfast.

But by then, Billy might be so far
down the road they'll never find him. Or he'll
turn somewhere he shouldn't, and get lost.

Henry keeps thinking—what should he do?
He looks back out the window, sees Billy turning
off the road, heading toward that old red barn.

Henry has to hurry. He gets dressed,
looks into the other ward—the man in white,
whoever he might be, is no longer there.

Even if the man came back
and Henry tried to tell him Billy was outside,
could he make him understand?

Henry is not even sure Billy's name is really Billy.
   That man is new here.
   He won't know anything about us.

Henry takes a deep breath and pushes
through the door,
leaving the book that props it open.

He walks down a set of stairs, opens a heavy door,
and steps outside. The door locks behind him.
The sun is higher in the sky, brighter now.

Henry runs to the row of trees, stays in their shadow
until he gets to the fence. He squeezes through the gap
and looks back to see if anyone is following him.

No, he's alone out on the road, just like he's imagined.
Except he isn't thinking about how long it would take
to walk home. He's only worried about Billy.

Good-natured, friendly, sweet—
all those things. But Billy can't find
his way to the meal place by himself.

If he gets lost—and he will get lost—
he'll be scared, and he won't know how to find
his way back. Henry knows they'll both

be punished. *No one will understand that I
was trying to help.* He'll have to think about that later.
He has to hurry up and find his friend.

LIKE A BROTHER

The snow that came down yesterday
has melted. The air is fresh and cool.
Henry walks fast to keep warm.

He takes a deep breath, and for a minute thinks
maybe he won't bring Billy back to Riverview.
When he finds him, they'll keep walking.

They'll walk to Henry's house. *Mama, Papa,
Molly,* he might say, *Billy is like my
little brother—can he live with us?*

His family would think about it
and figure out a way for Henry to stay home
where he belongs. And Billy, too.

But right now, out here on his own—
this road looks longer than it did to Henry
from the window by his bed.

ON A DUSTY HAY BALE

Henry sees the old barn up ahead
where the road climbs a little hill.
He keeps walking until he reaches it.
A farmhouse behind the barn
has a light on in a downstairs window.
A kitchen, Henry guesses—he pictures a family:
Mama making pancakes, sister and Papa
at the table, eating them. With maple syrup,
maybe blueberries. He smells bacon—
is it real or is he dreaming?

Now he's hungry, getting scared—
for Billy, who might be lost, and for himself.
Because what will happen if it's Barker
who finds out he's gone?
A door into the barn is halfway open.
Henry slips inside to have a look around.
Dark. Abandoned. No animals—
except a spider, whose web breaks
across Henry's face. The spider drops
onto his arm, and Henry speaks to it:

I'm sorry, Spider. Have you seen my friend?
He sets the spider gently down

and peers into the darkness. As his eyes
adjust, he finds patches of light.
A rusty old tractor. A coil of rope.
An upside-down metal bucket.
Something gray-green in a dark corner?
    Yes—it's Billy.
    Curled up on a dusty hay bale.
        Sobbing.

HENRY WILL KNOW

Billy shakes and shudders and finally
stops crying. What is Henry doing here?
He reaches out for his friend's hand
and Henry takes it, pulls him to his feet.

He has to get him out of here.
Billy probably wishes he had never
left the ward, and now that he's walked
this far, he won't know how to get back.

It's a good thing I came, Henry thinks.
I'm scared too, but at least I know the way.
Billy goes with him, out of the barn, onto the road.
No one sees the two boys heading back to Riverview.

Henry keeps worrying about what will happen
when they get there. Even if he tried
to tell someone the whole story,
they still might think he ran away with Billy.

He remembers James that time: the bruises
on his face when four men brought him back.
The long hallway lined with chairs.
The straps.

Henry has counted to a hundred twice,
plus sixty-one more days, and Ted
is still strapped down. *Come on, Billy.*
We have to get back before they miss us.

HAS ANYONE COUNTED?

Henry doesn't know who decides
how to punish someone. He hopes he can
sneak back in with Billy and pretend they never
left. There aren't so many attendants on the ward
these days. Where would they be right now?

Have the boys lined up for breakfast?
Has anyone counted, and noticed that
two boys are missing? Is someone
out here, looking for them? Henry thinks
about all this on the way back to Riverview.

He and Billy slip inside the fence as the other boys
are walking in a line from their building
to the breakfast place. Wait—something is not
the same as usual. Twice as many boys,
and only one attendant, not two.

Is that the same one Henry saw early this morning?
Dark brown hair, wearing white. The man
is at the front of the long line. No one at the back.
Henry waits until no one is looking. Then he and Billy
get at the back of the line and walk in to breakfast.

HOW LONG WOULD IT TAKE?

The young, dark-haired attendant
looks puzzled. Worried.
  He's counting all of us,
  over and over again, Henry sees.

At the end of breakfast, Billy
helps Henry carry plates
back to the kitchen as if nothing
unusual has happened.

They walk to their building, the man in white
unlocks the door to their ward,
and Henry and Billy step back in.
The book is no longer holding the door open.

Henry is pretty sure this new attendant
can't tell the boys apart yet.
He knows that won't last long.
  Now's my chance, he thinks.

  Could I set Ted free? We could run away
  and go to my house. How long would it take
  for anyone to miss us?
  Could we take Billy with us?

No.
Ted can't run fast.
It's too far. Too cold.
Billy would be scared when it got dark.

Henry comes to understand—he won't
really do this. Because:
> *What if Billy gets outside the fence again*
> *and I'm not here? What if he got lost*
> *and no one found him?*

SOMETHING DIFFERENT

The new attendant is a quiet one.
Henry wonders why he wears
white clothes instead of dark blue
like the others. Did he notice
that two extra boys were in the line
going back from breakfast?

He has a little notebook, and he speaks
to each boy, then writes something down.

When he sees that Henry doesn't hear,
he kneels down to look at him, points
to himself and slowly moves his mouth, pulling
his teeth over his bottom lip, then touching
his tongue behind his teeth and making an O shape
with his lips. He points to Henry, raising his eyebrows.

It's a question, Henry sees.
    This man—Victor?—is trying to learn our names.

He looks carefully
at Victor's friendly face and decides
he'll try to tell him:
        My name is Henry.
Victor nods
and writes something in his notebook.

VICTOR THINKS ABOUT HIS WORK

1.

Victor thinks about the boys on the ward as he walks
back to his sleeping quarters. Which ones can feed
and dress themselves? Who requires help? A few need
to be watched so they don't try to flush their socks
to make the toilets overflow. Most can speak. One or two know
how to read a little bit, at least enough to enjoy
the Sunday funnies. Henry, a sweet-tempered boy,
has only spoken once—to say his own name. Although
he doesn't seem to hear, and rarely speaks, he has a friend
out in the hallway. Attendants who've been here a while say
that Henry's friend is prone to violence and must be
restrained at all times. But does that child have to spend
his whole life in a chair? *He might lash out again,* they
warn. Victor has his doubts. He decides to wait and see.

2.

A smaller boy with curly hair stays close by
Henry all the time and tugs on his arm
to let him know if someone yells or an alarm
goes off. Victor thinks the little guy
might be the ears, while Henry is the brains
of their two-person team. He could swear they
were not in line for breakfast that first day—
but how could they suddenly appear? That remains
a stubborn puzzle. One he has no time to solve.

He's too busy doing all that is expected of him—
sweeping the ward floor, laundering soiled sheets,
breaking up fights while keeping his resolve
to be non-violent. Plus the hygiene routines: help trim
all those toenails; see that the boys brush their teeth.

DON'T DO THAT

As Victor straps Ted into his chair each morning,
Henry stands by, watching. Once, when no one else
seems to be listening, he says,
    Don't do that.
Victor looks like he'd like to hear more,
but Henry can't say all that he's thinking:

> *My friend doesn't need to be strapped down like this.*
> *Sure, he whacked someone with a broom one time,*
> *but that man deserved it! I bet no one else remembers*
> *why they do this to Ted. Whenever someone new*
> *came in, the ones who were already here*
> *showed the new one how to tighten all the straps.*
>
> *And now, Ted doesn't try to fight it. He sits there*
> *while you do what someone told you to. He doesn't bang*
> *his fist against his chair until his knuckles get all bloody,*
> *like he did at first. He doesn't rock back and forth so hard*
> *the chair tips on its side. It used to take two men*
> *to strap him in—sometimes three—now one man can do it.*

Which is good in one way,
Henry realizes,

because now
there's only one man
doing all the work
that six men did before.

ANOTHER SPIDER

One morning, Victor watches a spider climb up
the pant leg of Henry's friend out in the hall.
Will he kick his leg to make the spider fall
to the floor, then stomp on it? No—he makes a cup
of his hand to protect the spider, and gives a shout
for Henry, who doesn't hear, of course, but then
Henry's little buddy tugs on his sleeve, and when
Henry sees the problem, he runs over. Without
the slightest hesitation, he picks up the spider, carries
it across the ward, opens the window an inch or so,
and lets the spider crawl over the windowsill
to get outside. Henry waits patiently, never hurries,
and Victor thinks, *It's as if this boy were a young CO.*
He already seems to know there is no need to kill.

WHY?

A sunny afternoon. Henry stands
at the window, looking at the sidewalk
and the grass below his window.

A cat stalks through tall weeds, catches
a mouse, tosses it in the air, chases
it, catches it again. Again.

On the sidewalk, Barker
is walking with Slim Jim when Victor
approaches, and they all come to a stop.

Why do the two men block Victor's way?
What are they talking about, with such
angry faces? Why does Slim Jim shove

Victor to the ground? Barker spits on him
and they both walk away. Henry tries
to understand. Tries and tries. Cannot.

TED SMILES

On the ward, Victor takes his time,
never rushing, never pushing,
never yelling at the boys.
He seems to like us, Henry notices. *He doesn't
slap us or pull us by our hair, or shove us out
the door if we're not moving fast enough.*

Henry sees how Victor talks to Ted
as he straps him to his chair each morning.
And one surprising morning, Ted
looks straight back at him and answers.
Henry wonders what Ted says that makes
Victor stop and loosen all the straps.

Even though the straps are looser, Ted still can't
get out and walk around. But he smiles at Victor,
and Victor smiles back. Henry speaks up:
He used to smile a lot. Victor looks at Henry, then at Ted,
and asks a question. Henry sees Ted talking
as he holds up a fistful of straps. He sees Victor thinking.

POLLY WOLLY DOODLE

Another new attendant comes.
Red hair sticks out above his ears.
Henry watches closely—will he be
like the old ones, or like Victor,
moving gently through the ward?

He wears white clothes like Victor. He smiles
and sometimes puckers up his lips and puffs
out his cheeks. *Whistling while he works,*
Henry remembers. *Long ago, Papa taught me,*
and Molly, too, how to whistle "Polly Wolly Doodle."

Henry tries to do that now. Some sound
must come out of him, and maybe
it's the song, because two boys stop and
look up, staring at a spot beyond Henry
as if they think someone is behind him, whistling.

Henry calls the new attendant "Whistler."

MUSIC

Three more old attendants leave. *(Goodbye, Baldy.)*
Three new ones come, and they all wear white
like Victor. Whistler brings a xylophone
onto the ward, and plays it in the hallway so that Ted
and other boys can listen. Henry sees Ted tilt his head
and start to tap his foot. Whistler lays the xylophone
across Ted's knees and puts the stick in his good hand,
inviting him to play. His straps get in the way,
so Victor unbuckles them and pushes them aside.
Ted smiles. Henry smiles. When Whistler puts
the xylophone away, no one straps Ted in again.

The next day, Victor doesn't strap Ted
into his chair. At first, Ted sits there anyway,
and Henry thinks,

> *He's used to that. I wonder*
> *what will happen*
> *if he gets up and walks away?*

Henry reaches out a hand—
Ted takes it, stands, and walks.
Barker comes in from another ward just then,
sees Ted walking free, and tries to get him
back into his chair. Will he pull the lever
calling other men to help? How many are still around?

Barker doesn't pull the lever. He looks at Victor,
who stands still, watching him. Ted goes and hides
behind Victor. Whistler comes and stands there too,
and then so do Henry and Billy.
Barker looks at them, shakes his head a little,
shrugs his shoulders, turns,
    and goes away.
Henry watches carefully.
Later on, he says to Ted, *Did anyone say anything?*
Ted shakes his head, *No.* Henry nods and says,
We all stood there together—and that was enough.

ALL THE THINGS HE'S MISSED

Henry has his friend back.
At first, Ted wobbles when he walks,
and Henry stands by in case he starts to fall.

Day by day, as Ted gets stronger, his walking steadies,
and it's not long before the two of them, along with Billy,
walk to meals together like they used to.

Henry shows Ted what he's missed, those months
he had to stay inside. *Be careful,* he says, pointing out
that the sidewalk crack is bigger than it used to be.

Ted tosses out some crumbs, and Henry remembers
how the chipmunks used to come when Ted did that.
He smiles when he sees that they still do.

A DEEP HOLE

What if it really is a graveyard?
Henry is watching the last snow of the season,
big flakes that melt before they hit the ground.

Across the road, two men are digging
a deep hole. They go away and come back
with a big box, put it in the hole, toss dirt on top,

and walk away. It happens again three days later.
Henry is confused:
>   *Those can't be graves,*
>   *because no one stands beside them singing*
>   *like we did for Mrs. Grayson.*

The next week it happens again,
only this time, the box is small.
>   *Are there little babies here? Did one get sick*
>   *and die? Where are the baby's parents?*
>   *Would someone tell my family if I died?*

QUESTIONS

It's been more than two years since we've
    been to visit Henry, Molly says. *His birthday*
        is next week—he'll be ten years old!

Papa hasn't ever been to Riverview.
    I've been working overtime, he says. *We can*
        afford three tickets. I'll pick them up tomorrow.

Mama and Papa sit together on the bus.
    In the seat behind them, Molly sits alone,
        thinking about Riverview and Henry.
Where does he sleep? What does he do all day?
    Who lives there with him? How tall is he now?
        Will he recognize me right away this time?

When they arrive at Riverview, she sees changes:
    Did the sidewalk have all these big cracks before?
        Why don't they rake up the old dead leaves?
She's sure the grass was mowed
    last time they were here. *Why is it so shaggy now?*
        She looks up at a broken window. *Wait—*

    could that be Henry looking out?

She hooks her arm through Papa's elbow,
  nervous now. Papa will be furious
      if he sees someone shoving Henry.
What will he do if someone jerks Henry
  through the door? Or yells at him
      as if that might make him hear?

Up the concrete stairs, through the heavy door,
  into the waiting room. The three of them
      wait and wait. And wait.
Does anyone even work here anymore? Mama asks.
  Papa says, *I've heard these places are understaffed,*
      because so many men have been drafted.

Finally, the door opens.
  A young man wearing white
      enters the room, approaches them,
and says, *Good afternoon. My name is Victor.*
  I understand you're here to visit Henry.
      Please wait. I'll bring him out to you.

HE BRACES HIMSELF

Henry's family seems friendly enough, even kind,
but Victor wonders if they know why he's
here at Riverview. If they have a loved one overseas,
as most families do, how will they react when they find
out he's a CO? He braces himself for the sting
of contempt that sometimes boils over into rage.
That girl, Henry's sister, must be about his age
or a few years younger. When he said he'd bring
Henry out, she smiled, and Victor could tell
she really loves her brother. As he combs Henry's hair,
and helps him clean up, Victor realizes he doesn't smell so
great himself. It's not exactly him, it's the smell
of Riverview. Isn't there a bar of decent soap somewhere?
Never mind. *Come on, Henry,* he motions, *let's go.*

OH, HENRY

Henry stares at his family
    as if coming into too-bright sunlight
      from a darkened room.
Mama reaches to embrace him.
    Even Papa fights back tears
      as he takes a long, deep breath.
Molly looks her brother up and down.
    He must be two inches taller.
      Scruffy-looking hair (though
he's tried to comb it). *Oh, Henry,* she says,
    and that reminds her—she smiles
      to herself—she's brought
a candy bar for him that has his name
    on it. She'll find it in a minute.
      But now they're being rude.
They should introduce themselves to the attendant.
    He seems nicer than the last one. Molly hopes so;
      she can't bear to see the expression she saw
last time they were here—that man who said *What?*
    in a mean way when he heard Henry talk.
      It makes her throat sting to recall it.
Is it really such a grand wish
    that someone here could simply see
      who her brother truly is?

It was as if I'd made a wish on a magic lamp,
    she'll think later, when she recalls
        this moment, how
she looked up that morning
    into the face of the young man
        and heard him speaking softly.
Hello, he says.
    You must be Henry's sister.

    Molly is so startled by his quiet voice
she barely hears him add,
    Your brother
        is my favorite.

FAMILY

Victor looks out the window, sees Henry between his mother
and his sister, who wears a yellow dress. When Henry links
his arms in theirs as they cross the grass, Victor thinks
of his own family. He is stabbed with longing for his brother
Steven, and for Joey and his parents, who,
like Henry's parents, would have brought a picnic basket
full of sandwiches, spread a blanket on the grass, cut
a slice of cake for each person. Henry's family's blue
blanket is like a patch of cloudless sky.
But Victor has to get back to work on the drab
and dirty ward. Impossible to keep it clean,
though he's determined not to give up. *Why
are there so few people working here? All I can do is grab
a mop and bucket. And try my best not to become mean.*

HAPPY BIRTHDAY

They've been saving up their ration points
    for everything they need to make a birthday cake.
        Mama opens up her basket
and there it is! Molly holds it out to Henry
    and he sees that it's for him. He hasn't had
        a birthday cake since he was six—how old is he now?
Papa puts candles on the cake, and Henry
    counts them—ten! Do these candles mean that he's
        almost as old as Molly now? No—she's older
too, of course. He sees his family deciding whether they
    should sing. They do. He knows how the song goes:
        Happy birthday, dear Henry, happy birthday to you.
He's supposed to blow out the candles now.
    He remembers something: a man trying to make him
        blow out candles when it wasn't anybody's birthday.
He still can't understand why that was so important.
    He knows one thing about birthday candles: before you blow,
        you make a wish. Easy—he wishes they would take him home.
He says it right out loud: *I want to go home.*
    He's sure they understand, but no one answers.
        He blows out all ten candles in one try. Then he asks:
Why do I have to stay here? Molly looks at him
    and says something to Mama and Papa. Does Papa
        say he's sorry? Henry thinks so, but he isn't sure.

Mama cuts a piece of cake for each of them.
It tastes the way Henry remembers from long ago,
and being with his family makes it taste even better.
But no one seems to be as happy as they were
before he said his wish. He's glad he said it,
even though he's pretty sure it won't come true today.

They didn't bring an orange—Henry asks
if he can have some cake to take
back to his friends.
He only meant to ask for two pieces, one for Ted
and one for Billy—but Mama gives him
all the cake left on the plate.

THE HEAVY DOOR

Molly hates this part, when they have to say goodbye,
    even this time, when the young attendant tries
        to be so kind. They're in the waiting room again,
and now it's time to leave. Victor comes through
    the heavy door, steps in front of Henry as a way
        of getting his attention. He simply smiles
and motions to the door. Henry understands this time,
    and follows. Molly tries to follow too—she wants
        to see where Henry spends his days. She offers
to help Henry take the cake to his friends. *I'll only
    stay a minute,* she tells Victor. *I can bring the plate
        back out.* Victor shakes his head.
I'm sorry. No. I'll bring the plate to you.
    Gently, he adds, *I'm glad you came to visit Henry.*
        Molly looks at him. *I'm Molly,* she says. *Thank you
for your kindness. We would come more often if we could,
    but it's hard to get time off and save up money
        for the bus.* Victor nods. *I understand.*
He opens the door, and Molly is almost knocked
    backward by the smell. Henry says, *Go back
        home now, Molly,* as the door shuts between them.

AFTER THEIR VISIT

1.

Henry goes about his days,
more peaceful now, knowing
he is not forgotten, though the food
at Riverview tastes worse than ever,
compared to the sweet birthday cake.

The hour of their picnic lingers in his mind—
cool lemonade, sandwiches, and carrot sticks.
And the memory of Molly's and Mama's arms
linked in his as they walked along the path together.

2.

Victor crosses the grass when his work
is finished for the day: a patch of dandelions—
flash of yellow, like a yellow dress—and there he is
again, thinking about that girl's sweet smile.

Molly. How she treated Henry. Respectful—as if,
in her eyes, there is nothing wrong with him.
Victor hopes she doesn't know
he's working here at Riverview
instead of being sent to prison.

HOLY, HOLY, HOLY

Victor looks around the ward, and his eyes
fall on the shabby covers on each bed,
green army blankets full of holes. Mother always said
to keep a sense of humor, and Victor tries—
he starts humming a hymn that comes to mind,
Holy, holy, holy . . . He smiles to himself, missing Steven,
who would have laughed out loud, even
at such a small joke. *Not,* Victor thinks, *just being kind,
either. He'd notice the same thing I do, and we'd laugh
together. Joey too, and Mother, though she'd think she
shouldn't.* He pictures her sitting in the lamplight
with Father. He knows he's luckier by far than half
the group of COs who have been sent here. When he
is certain all the boys are sleeping, he sits down to write.

Dear Folks,

It's quiet now as I sit down to write. "Dear Folks"
does not begin to say how glad I am that I have your
support. We're not all so lucky. I've met twelve more
COs here. Jon, who works on the next ward over, pokes
his head into our ward every now and then, and we've
become friends. He told me his parents were so
upset when they found out he was a CO
that they disowned him. I find this hard to believe,
but he said his mother told the girl he was
engaged to, "Don't marry my cowardly son."
He's still not sure what the girl is going to do.
Well, it's late. Just wanted to write because
I haven't heard from you (or Steven, since that one
letter from boot camp). I have been thinking of you.

>   With love,
>   Victor

Dear Victor,

Thank you for writing. We have been thinking of you,
too. I don't know which is worse, Steven fighting this war
that seems to go on and on, only getting bigger, or
you in that awful place. Son, you are contributing too,
in spite of what people say. Someone threw a rotten egg
on our front porch last night, and left this note:
"For you and your conchie son. He'll be able to vote
one day, just as if he'd given an arm and a leg
for his country, like real American boys and men."
Maybe we shouldn't tell you this—I suppose I ought
to write of pleasant things. But when I lie awake
at night, my mind goes back to my brother. When
he died, and your father lost his arm, we thought
it was "to end all war." How much will this war take?

    With love,
      Mother

NOVEMBER 7, 1943

Dear Father and Mother,

Cockroaches climb up and down the wall.
I try not to see them. I need
to keep my mind on what I'm doing as I feed
Josiah, who can't feed himself, while I watch all
the others, making sure each of them has time
to finish eating, and that no one tries to steal
another's food. I had no time to deal
with sticky tabletops today. The grime
that coats the floor has been there so long
I'm not sure it can ever be cleaned up.
Today I overheard the mumbled words of a man
who's worked here for ten years: "These kids belong
in a zoo." I simply stated, "That's not true." I held a cup
for Josiah, gave him a drink of water. I do what I can.

With love,
Victor

TRYING NOT TO SPILL

Henry and Ted watch Victor, helping if they can.
They see how Josiah tries hard not to spill,
but even with Victor steadying his arm, he can't
control the way his hand jerks out on its own
and sometimes knocks things over. Henry thinks,
These new attendants don't punish us
for every little thing we might do wrong.

Josiah finishes his lunch, leans back on the bench,
rocking. Then the boys line up and start to walk
back to the ward. Halfway there, Josiah stumbles
and falls into the boy ahead of him,
who whirls around with a raised fist.
Victor holds up one hand and speaks quietly:
Take it easy, my friend.

The boy lowers his fist and they walk on.
A peace treaty witnessed by forty boys
and two passing squirrels.

THROAT BURNING
JANUARY 1944

Henry wakes up in the middle of the night,
his throat burning as if he's swallowed soup
before it cooled. His nightshirt is
completely soaked. His head hurts,
and he aches all over.

He stays in his bed, waiting
for someone to come. Memories flood in
from somewhere long ago: an earache,
a cold sweat, and his throat hurt like this.
Papa put a big, warm hand
on my forehead, he remembers.
Mama washed my face
with a cool washcloth.
When it got warm, she dipped it
in cold water, wrung it out,
and put it on my face again.

Victor is alone on the ward, and has
three other wards to keep an eye on.
Finally, he comes in and walks along
the rows of beds. Henry is crying now,
and Victor comes to see what's wrong.
My throat hurts, Henry tells him. Victor

brings a drink of water, and even though
it's the middle of the night, he gets out
Henry's day clothes, and Henry
puts them on. Victor finds a sheet of paper,
shows Henry how to fold it back and forth
to make a fan and fan himself. Then he gestures
to let Henry know, *I have to get someone to stay
here with the others. I'll be right back.*
Henry fans himself and waits for Victor.
When he comes back with Whistler,
Whistler stays on the ward, and Victor
walks with Henry through the cool night air
to another building, where they enter a clean room.

Henry takes it all in:
A woman wearing a white cap and apron.
Two rows of beds—eight beds in each row,
and no one sleeping in any of them.
Stacks of white cloth folded into little squares.
He gets into the bed they take him to.
It smells nicer than his other bed.

The woman
then gives him a white pill with a glass of cool water.
He drinks it and falls asleep.

FOUR DAYS, THREE NIGHTS

Henry wakes and looks around, unsure
of where he is. His throat still burns;
his head and arms and legs ache.
A nurse brings him more water.
It's hard to swallow, but he drinks
the water and goes back to sleep.

Wakes up. Sleeps. Again. Light, dark.
Hot, cold. He dreams that Molly dives into
a lake and beckons to him: *Come on in.*
He steps into the water, and it's cool.
When he wakes up, he's not quite so hot.

When he came here,
these other beds did not have boys in them.
Now they do. And in the bed across from his bed—
there is Billy, sleeping, his face red
and puffed up like a chipmunk
with its cheeks full of acorns.
What does his own face look like?
He hopes Billy doesn't feel the way
he felt when he came here. He hopes
his friend will wake up soon and smile.

But that does not happen. Before
Billy wakes up, Victor comes
with clean clothes for Henry
and takes him back to his ward.

TOO MANY DAYS

Five beds on the ward are empty now—
Billy's and four others.
   Henry wonders,
   Is Billy still in the place
   where I slept when I was sick?
One by one, the other boys come back.
Henry points to Billy's bed and asks Victor,
   Where is Billy? When will he come back?
   Victor turns his head to the side
   and leans it on his hands.
He closes his eyes.
Henry doesn't know what that means.
   Is Billy still sleeping
   in that room
   that smelled so clean?
More days go by. Too many.
Henry is as sick
   with worry
   as he was
   with fever.

USUALLY NO FAMILY

Henry watches out the window:
men dig more holes
and bury boxes in them.

A graveyard. He is sure of it.

Every day
a new grave.
    Sometimes two.
    Usually no family or friends
    come to stand beside the graves
    when these boxes are lowered
    into the earth.

Henry has a feeling
that makes his stomach hurt.
    He doesn't have the words he needs
    to ask if what he fears
    is true.

Dear Mr. and Mrs. Williams,

The director asked me to write to you about your son.
Henry is doing okay now, but he's had a rough time because
of a mumps epidemic that went through the ward. He was
the first to get it, followed by twelve other boys, and one,
I'm very sorry to tell you, has died. He was Henry's friend,
and I'm not sure how much Henry understands. One day
he pointed at the empty bed, and I think he tried to say
the boy's name. Then he started crying. You may wish to send
something to cheer him up. A comic book, perhaps, or
a tablet of drawing paper with crayons or a pencil. Most
of the boys don't have families who visit or write to them—
Henry is one of the lucky ones. I'm sure you know how much your
visit meant to him, and though I understand the high cost
of bus fares, I hope you'll find a way to come again and see him.

Sincerely,
Victor Jorgensen

Dear Mr. Jorgensen,

It is kind of you to write to us. We have all
been so worried about Henry, and now
your letter gives us a better idea of how
we can help. We wanted to visit again last fall,
but we had too many other expenses, and we could
not make it. The winter has been difficult. My father
was sick. He is much better now—I won't bother
you with details. My mother hurt her hand, or she would
answer. She has asked me to write this letter
to send with our gifts for Henry. Could you
please give him the tablet and crayons now,
and save the comic book for later? It's better
that way—instead of one present, he'll have two.
We do want to visit, but at this time we can't see how.

Sincerely,

Molly Williams

FAMILIES

Henry misses Billy, and he can tell
Ted does too, because one day after lunch
he found a scrap of paper and drew a picture
that looked just like Billy.

Henry wishes they had better paper
and more pencils, and then one day, they do!
Victor brings a tablet and crayons
and to let Henry know who sent them,
he opens the crayons and starts drawing on the tablet.
He draws a man with brown hair and a beard,
wearing a plaid shirt.
    Papa, Henry says.
Then a woman in a blue dress, smiling.
    Mama.
Henry takes the yellow crayon from the box,
and gives it to Victor, who nods and smiles—
he remembers Molly's yellow dress.
He draws Henry's sister, holding out the tablet.
Beside the three of them, he draws a smaller boy—
Henry, with the box of crayons in his hand.

Henry holds up the picture
to show Ted, who studies it and says

something to Victor. Victor starts to draw again:
a man wearing white—Henry thinks
he's drawn a picture of himself. Beside him,
a boy about the size of Ted and Henry.
On his other side, he draws a tall young man, a soldier.
    You have two brothers? Henry asks.
    Yes, Victor nods. Henry points to each one:
    Younger. Older. You.
Then Victor draws his parents.
His mother wears a green dress
and a flowered apron, his father a blue shirt
with one sleeve folded and pinned up.

Ted looks at the picture for a long time,
points to the picture of that sleeve,
then to his own arm, hanging loosely at his side.
Victor and Ted have a conversation, and Henry
wonders what it is about.
    Maybe Victor is saying that his father
    has a missing arm, a little bit like Ted.

EMPTY BED

Henry points to Billy's empty bed
and draws a picture that he hopes
Victor will recognize as Billy.

Where is my friend? he asks.
Victor leans his head on his hands again,
closes his eyes.

Henry doesn't know what this means.
He hopes it means that Billy is still
sleeping in that room where he last saw him.

But in the back of Henry's mind,
this thought gets bigger:
    No one else was there this long.

ALMOST FOR SURE

Billy does not come back. A new boy
    comes, and they give him Billy's bed—
    that's when Henry knows, almost for sure,
that Billy died. For a while, he reasons,
    Maybe he went home, like I keep hoping
    I will. But then he thinks of how he saw
men digging holes and putting boxes in them
    in the place that brings a stinging memory:
    the graveyard where we buried Mrs. Grayson.
Except here there is no one
    to sing or cry beside the graves.
    No stones or monuments to mark them.

Dear Mr. and Mrs. Williams and Molly,

Yesterday, Henry asked me to send
these drawings to you. I'm not sure what they
are. Do you recognize the woman with gray
hair up in a bun, wearing a red dress? I won't pretend
I can interpret this, but the second picture could
be the little boy I told you about, who died
around the same time Henry was so sick. I'd
say the third one is a rock. With scratches on it? Would
you possibly be able to guess what could be
on Henry's mind? He's been drawing pictures, one
or two each day, hiding them under his mattress to keep
them safe. Yesterday he gave these three to me
to send to you. He drew a picture of your family with the sun
shining on you—he likes to look at it before he goes to sleep.

Sincerely,
Victor Jorgensen

COULD THIS BE MRS. GRAYSON?

Henry's drawings, spread across the table,
    bring light to this dark room. Molly tries
        to imagine he is here with them. Mama asks,
Could this be Mrs. Grayson? Remember?
    She often wore a bright red dress.
        Molly does not remember that. *How,*
she asks, *would Henry remember something I don't?*
    Mama thinks about this as she looks at the pictures.
        Mrs. Grayson loved our Henry. Toward the end,
she couldn't get around much. I'd take Henry
    over to her house and he would cheer her up
        with his sweet smiles. She died when he was
three—she never knew he became deaf.
    Papa says, *I'd be surprised if he remembers her,*
        but you never know. As Molly stretches her mind
around their words, a memory floats up: *We took him*
    to her funeral. I remember . . . he couldn't understand
        what dying meant, and he asked a lot of questions,
especially about the gravestones. We told him
    they help us remember people after they're gone.
        Mr. Grayson played "Swing Low, Sweet Chariot"
on his harmonica, and we all sang together.
    Remember how much Henry loved to sing?
        Mama says, *Victor might be right.*

What if Henry knows his friend died
  and worries that everyone will forget him? Would
      Henry expect to have a funeral and see a gravestone?

After a long silence, Papa says, *They can't afford*
  to have funerals and gravestones for everyone
      who dies at Riverview. Molly stares at her parents.
If it happened to Henry, she says, *we'd have a funeral.*
  We'd go get him and bring him home and bury him
      by Grandpa and Grandma. Or next to Mrs. Grayson.
We would put a marker on his grave.
  Of course we would!
      Papa?
      Mama?
      Wouldn't we?

Neither of them answers. Mama's face is tight,
  like it is when they have to say goodbye to Henry.
      Let's pray it will never come to that, she says at last.
Molly says, *What?*
  And Mama adds, in a quiet voice: *We would find a way*
      to do what needed to be done.
Papa tries to explain:
  You know how hard it is
      for us to get there, Molly.
Many families live even farther from Riverview
  than we do. Remember what Victor Jorgensen wrote
      in his first letter? Most children never hear from

their families once they're left at Riverview.

Molly blinks back tears. *At least,* says Papa, *we can visit
Henry once a year or so.* Molly keeps her voice
as calm and steady as she can. She stands up
and replies: *It's not just Henry. It's all of them.*
She holds up Henry's picture. *Who is this little boy?*

*Papa, I can get a job after school. Mama, I don't need
a new coat—I'll lengthen my old brown one.
We have to visit Henry.
Soon.*

MAY 1, 1944

Dear Victor,

Thank you for sending Henry's pictures. We think
you must be right. The woman wearing red
died when Henry was three. My parents said
that she loved Henry. He would go over and drink
hot chocolate with her, and he liked to sing
with her and her husband—when he could still hear,
of course. Do you know, or can you find out, where
his friend is buried? We'd like to do something
to help Henry understand what happened. He
may want to have a funeral. Victor, do you ever
get a day off? If you could let us know, we might
be able to visit on that day, and if you have time, we
could do something so Henry knows that little boy will never
be forgotten. It is getting late here—I will say good night.

Your friend,
Molly Williams

A KNOT OF JOY

It's still dark when Molly and her parents
    get on the Greyhound bus. A light rain
        is falling, and the driver says,
Shake out your umbrellas
    before you get on—
        helps keep the aisles dry.

Molly sits behind her parents—she has two
    seats to herself until they stop for breakfast.
        Then a man in uniform embraces a young woman,
gets on, and takes the empty seat.
    He doesn't talk. He falls asleep and snores.
        Good. She doesn't want a stranger asking
where she's going today, or who they're visiting,
    or why they'll have to catch the bus back home
        just four short hours after they arrive.

It's not that she's ashamed, exactly.
    It's just that everything someone might ask
        about this trip—about Henry—is so private.

She's glad the soldier stays asleep
    through the city and all the little towns,
        until the bus arrives in front of Riverview.

It isn't raining here. A few crocuses are up.

A knot of joy—Henry!—leaps in Molly's heart. She tries not to let these dark brick buildings weigh it down.

LIKE THE KITCHEN USED TO SMELL

Henry is looking out the window.
  What's going on in the big tree today?
  Two squirrels on one branch, a red bird
  on another. Now here comes the bus
  with the gray dog painted on its side,
  running fast like it always does.
And then the bus stops and he sees them—
  Molly! Mama! And Papa has come again.
  They have parcels in their hands!
  Victor isn't on the ward, but Whistler comes
  with clean clothes and good shoes,
  and he takes Henry to the visiting room.
Henry sits down with his family. Mama opens her bag
  and takes out treats: raisin cookies, apples,
  and sandwiches made out of bread that tastes
  like the kitchen used to smell. Henry remembers
  Mama standing by the stove in her apron.
  She's put apple butter on his sandwich.
He remembers the smell of apple butter, and wishes
  he'd saved the last few pages of his tablet
  so he could draw the apple tree in the backyard.
  And then, just as he wishes that, Molly
  takes out a new tablet and gives it to him.
  Papa gives him two new pencils. And an orange!

He isn't sure if he should peel it now or save it
to share with Ted. He decides to peel it
and give some to his sister. But when he offers Molly
half the orange, she looks like she might cry.
Does she want the whole orange? *Here, Molly,*
Henry says, *you can have it.* Why do tears
spill down his sister's cheeks when he says that?

IN A FRAME, PROTECTED

Victor enters the visiting room, and Henry asks,
    Why are you here? Victor looks at Molly, smiles
    as she opens her bag and takes out the pictures
    Victor sent them. Henry blinks hard. *Did you*
    understand? he asks his family. *My friend died.*
    I don't want to forget him. Mama nods.
She has a photograph of Mrs. Grayson.
    When she puts it beside Henry's drawing,
    his whole face lights up. *Yes!* he says.
    Victor talks to Henry's family—
    they seem to have some kind of secret.
    Henry watches closely.
They walk outside together, past the place
    where Victor got pushed down that time,
    past the bus stop. They cross the road.
    Victor has a key that opens a gate
    to the place where Henry has seen
    men digging holes for all those boxes.

Rows of metal sticks with little marks
    on them: Molly sees they are not
    names, but numbers. Victor stops
    at number 124 and kneels to brush

away some muddy leaves. Molly
     wishes Henry could hear her say,
This is why we're here today.
     She takes out Henry's drawing
     of the boy with curly hair: his friend.
     She has put it in a frame with glass,
     and they prop it up against the 124 stick.
     Molly rests her hand on Henry's shoulder.
Yes! Thank you! His answer bubbles up.
     They've understood. The five of them stand
     together, around the grave, and Victor writes
     a name on a stone beside the number stick,
Who is this little boy? asks Molly.
     Victor looks down at the grave and speaks.
I don't know much about him, only that
     he came here shortly after he was born,
     the youngest of eight children. His record says
     he was on the infant and toddler ward
     for four years before he came to ours.
     It describes him as unteachable.

Henry wonders what Victor has said
     that makes Molly and Mama cry.

Papa gestures toward Henry,
     inviting him to speak.
     Henry stands up straight and tall, while
     Mama, Papa, Molly, and Victor bow their heads.

He was my friend, Henry says.

When he smiled, everyone felt happy.

Then Henry's family and Victor sing together.

FOREVER?

Going home, Molly sits with Papa.
    He lets her have the window seat,
        and Mama takes the seat across from them.
They ride in thoughtful silence
    as the sun gets lower in the sky,
        then briefly brightens the horizon
before disappearing altogether. The bus
    heads south and darkness settles in.
        Does Henry have to stay at Riverview forever?
Molly thinks about this for a long time before
    asking Papa, who seems so sorrowful
        she wants to pull the question back.
It hangs there in the dark, unanswered.
    Papa gets up to help a young mother
        with her suitcase, and when the mother's
baby starts to cry, Mama says, *I'll hold him.*
    Molly watches Mama comfort
        the sweet baby. Is she remembering
how she once held Henry just like that?

NOT ENOUGH

JUNE 1944

More boys arrive.
They have to push the beds together
and move the cabinets to one end
of the ward to make room for everyone.
At mealtime, there is never
enough food on their plates.

The men who wear white
work side by side with
the few who wear blue—
Henry thinks the blue ones
have become a little nicer,
but there aren't enough
of any of them, anywhere.

Ever since Baldy left, no one
takes the boys outdoors to play.
There wouldn't be time, anyway, because
any boys like Ted and Henry who are capable
of helping have so much work to do:
scrub the stairwells, mow the grass,
peel potatoes, sweep the ward.

Victor and Whistler start a garden.
It's hours and hours of work, but Henry
likes it better than the indoor work.
Digging in dirt, planting seeds, then watering
the new green sprouts as they grow bigger.
After a while, there are peas to pick, then
beans and squash. Tomatoes,
lettuce, radishes. From garden
to kitchen, to everyone's plates.
  The work and the food
  make Henry happy.

SO SMART!

Some evenings, after all the boys
are in bed, Victor takes out a deck of cards
and sits down at a little table. Henry thinks,
  That looks like a game you play by yourself.
Sometimes when he can't sleep, he gets up,
and if everyone else is sleeping,
Victor lets him sit down at the table.

Henry sees how it works: Red on black.
King, queen, jack. He studies the cards:
diamond and heart shapes,
spades and three-leaf clovers.
Only one big shape on some of them,
up to ten on others. Victor tries
to get them in a certain order.

He shuffles them and Henry watches
as he sets them up and turns them over,
one at a time, looking at each one.
Henry sees how Victor moves
diamonds to diamonds, clovers to clovers,
hearts to hearts, spades to spades—
each stack in order, starting with the smallest.

Sometimes Victor shakes his head as if he's
disappointed, and puts the cards back in their box.
Sometimes he mixes them up again
and starts over. Once in a while, he gets the cards
just how he wants them. He picks them
up and taps them on the table, smiling,
then shuffles them and starts the game all over.

One night Victor is staring at the cards,
thinking hard. Henry sees that he's
about to give up, and he points
to a card with three diamonds on it—
then shows Victor a place it could go
so the cards are in the right order. Victor
stares at the cards, and at Henry—*so smart!*

Dear Mr. and Mrs. Williams and Molly,

As you have heard in the letter the director sent out
last week, they have changed the name of this place
to "Riverview State Training School." In case
you have any doubts, there is nothing about
Henry that has ever been at all "feebleminded." That
name change (for everyone here) is long overdue.
Now they hope to train some boys at Riverview
in skills that might allow them to go home. What
do you see as Henry's future? To be quite
honest, there isn't much training going on here.
If it were possible, would you want to find a way
for Henry to be discharged? He is so intelligent! In spite
of our best efforts, the overcrowding here is severe,
and it's hard to give even the most basic care each day.

Your friend, on Henry's side,
Victor Jorgensen

WE'VE ALWAYS KNOWN

The first red roses climb the trellis
    on the day Victor's letter arrives.
        Molly opens it, and reads as she walks
from the mailbox to the house, stumbling
    over a stick, catching her balance, then
        running, breathless, into the kitchen
waving the letter at her parents:
    Henry is not *unteachable. Victor says*
        he's smart, just like we've always known.
Papa reaches for the letter, and Mama
    comes to look over his shoulder. Molly says,
        The School for the Deaf is closer than
Riverview—maybe they'll let Henry go there now.
    Papa says, *I don't know, Molly. Would they*
        accept a child his age who has missed out
on his first five years of school? Molly says, *He could*
    start in first grade. Papa looks doubtful,
        but there's so much hope on Molly's face,
he finally says, *I suppose we could ask.*

Mama stares hard at the two of them.
    You can ask if you want to, she says. *I will*
        never set foot in that place again.

They insulted Henry. They insulted me.
   They wouldn't listen to reason or give him
      a second chance. As awful as Riverview is,
I'd leave him there before I'd take him
      back to that school. Molly picks up the letter
         and reads it again, more carefully.
Victor isn't asking us to tell him
      where Henry would go next, she says. *He only*
         wants to know if we would like to get him out
of Riverview. Mama does not reply, so Molly presses on:
      Let's bring him home and then decide, she begs.
         Wouldn't he be better off at home than he is there?
Mama replies, *He couldn't be much worse.*
   They stop talking, then, but keep on
      thinking.

THEY SHOULD HAVE BEEN ASHAMED

Molly walks slowly on her way to school
   remembering the boys who were so mean
      when she was younger, how they teased her
about Henry—why did they do that? She has no wish
   to be friends with them, even though
      they've long since stopped their teasing.

When Henry had to go away, did any of them care?
   She doubts it. Only one of them,
      a boy named Bobby, ever said he was sorry,
and by that time, it was too late to apologize to Henry.
   They're the ones who should be ashamed.
      Not me. Not Henry. Molly knows that much
for sure by now, but still, she never
   talks to anyone outside her family
      about Henry.
Maybe, she thinks, *it's time to start.*
   Because if he does come home, she wants him
      to be welcomed back.

THE SAME FIVE PEOPLE

Victor teaches Ted and Henry
    two new card games. He shows
        Henry how to shuffle—Ted lets Henry
do that part, but both boys catch on fast
    to how the games work. Now they have something
        new to do when they get their work done.
And if they're tired of playing cards, they can draw
    on Henry's tablet. Ted likes to draw a big house
        with a porch, the same five people, same black dog.
Henry feels like he knows Ted's family.
    The house looks fancier than the house
        Henry lived in long ago. He wonders if
he'll ever see that house again. He draws it
    as he remembers, line by line, windows,
        door, garden, flowers by the gatepost.
Papa, Mama, Molly, and himself. The more he draws,
    the more he remembers—the neighbor with her baby,
        the dog across the street that scared him when it growled.

WHERE IS TED?

JULY 1944

Henry, watching out the window, sees
a car drive up. A man and a woman get out, and then
Whistler comes in with clean clothes and shoes.

Someone on the ward has visitors. Henry knows
it isn't him, and hopes it's Ted, because when Ted
gets treats, he brings them back and shares them.

It *is* Ted! Whistler takes him out—to the nice room,
Henry knows that much. He can't wait
for Ted to come back with an orange.

At lunch, Henry sits alone. He walks
back without a partner, hoping Ted will be
on the ward by the time he gets back.

He isn't. Henry waits and waits.
  He should be here by now, he thinks.
  Surely by now . . . Where is he?

Whistler comes in and takes the sheets
off Ted's bed. It's not sheet-changing day—
what's wrong? Did Ted have to go to that place

you go when you are sick? Oh no!
Henry looks out the window. The car is gone.
If he was right, and Ted's parents came—

where is Ted? Victor comes in to take the boys
to supper, and when they all line up, and Ted
is still not back, Henry points to Ted's bed

and asks, *Where is he?* Victor looks at Henry,
tries to answer slowly, carefully. But Henry
can't understand what he is saying.

WHAT IS GOING ON?

Ted doesn't come back. A new boy comes
and sleeps in Ted's bed. Did Ted's family
bury him in that graveyard with Billy?

No—people get sick first, before
they die. Ted wasn't sick. That morning, before
he disappeared, they'd just played a card game.

Henry almost won, but then Ted did something
really smart, and he beat Henry. He was not
at all sick. So what is going on?

Victor brings a map, and points to different spots
on it, but Henry has never seen a map before.
He can't figure out what Victor wants to tell him.

Maybe he should try
to find a new friend,
but he sure doesn't feel like it.

HENRY FIGURES IT OUT

It rains for six days straight. Then the sun comes out,
and that same day, Victor strides in,
smiling, with a letter in his hand.

He gives it to Henry, and Henry sees an *H*
on the envelope. It's for him! It's different
from the letters Molly and his parents send,
always in square brown envelopes
with pictures inside, drawings of their house
and garden. Sometimes a Christmas tree.

This letter is in a long white envelope. Henry is careful
not to tear it when he opens it—inside is
a picture, but it's not from Molly.

It's just like the pictures Ted was always drawing—
that same house, with people standing out in front of it.
Only in this picture, the tree beside the house is bigger,
and instead of five people, there are six. No black dog,
but a little brown one. Henry figures it out: The sixth person
is Ted. The black dog ran away or died, and they got a new one.

Yes. Of course.
It must be true:
Ted got to go home!

Dear Mr. Jorgensen,

Yes, we would be interested in anything you could
tell us about how we might bring our Henry home.
You're right: he is intelligent. We have always known
he's as smart as a whip—if he could hear, he would
do very well in school. Maybe you know about the School
for the Deaf—he refused to take their "test," so he was sent
to Riverview. After your letter came, my husband went
over to that school to speak to the principal—a fool
of a man—who said Henry cannot apply again. "It's too
late. He is older, and he would be too far behind
the other students his age." They'll never admit he's
always been as "teachable" as any child. We thank you
for noticing that, and yes, we would like to find
out what we need to do next. Tell us, please.

Sincerely,

Martha Williams

HE'S GOOD AT DRAWING

Molly makes up her mind:
    she will start talking about Henry—
        at school and anywhere in town
where people may (or may not)
    remember him. She wants everyone
        to know he might be coming back.

If he does come home, she's determined to find a way
    to teach him everything she's learned in school
        during the five years he's been gone.

He can see, she reasons, *and he's*
    good at drawing. He obviously remembers
        what words mean and how they sound.
So why not try to teach him to read and write?
    I could show him pictures, and teach him the alphabet.
        And then we can write words to describe the pictures.

She draws pictures to send to Henry, showing him
    what has changed at home, so he won't be
        too surprised: the lilac bush is bigger now,
and Papa built a footbridge across the creek.
    Henry will not know that Snowball, who was
        just a kitten when he left, has three new kittens

of her own, born beside the kitchen stove last week.
She wonders if her brother will be home
by the time the apples are ready to be picked.

AUDREY AND MELINDA

As Molly is mailing her picture to Henry,
    she sees two cheerful women sorting mail
        at a table in the back of the post office.
They seem to be talking to each other
    without speaking out loud. She asks the clerk
        who they are, and he says, *They're sisters,*
Audrey and Melinda Bradley. Audrey,
    the one in the blue dress, is deaf.
        They've been in town all their lives,
but this is the first time they've had jobs.
    So many of our employees are fighting
        overseas, and we need extra help.
These two sisters showed us that either one of them
    can sort the mail, and the two of them together
        can sort it twice as fast. So we hired them both.

Molly can't stop staring at them.
    Why do they keep moving their hands
        like that? she asks. *It's some kind*
of sign language, says the clerk. *Not sure*
    how or where they learned it. Melinda can
        interpret anything we say, for Audrey.

Molly walks home thinking:

If I can learn that sign language, and Henry
learns it too, we could talk again,
just like we did when we were little. I could tell him
what other people are saying, and then he could
answer in words or signs or both.
Then I'll show him how
to read and write. Henry can
learn anything he wants to.

WE CAN TEACH YOU

It seems to Molly that the world is spinning faster
    since they decided to bring Henry home.
        The next time she's in the post office,
she says to the clerk—*If those two sisters aren't too busy,*
    could you tell them that I'd like to meet them?
        They come out to the front and Molly says,
My name is Molly Williams.
    My brother Henry is deaf, and doesn't talk much.
        He's been gone since he was six years old,
and he'll be coming home soon. I was wondering
    if you can teach us how to talk to each other.
        Melinda signs to Audrey and they both smile.
Then Audrey folds her hand into a soft fist
    and moves it up and down. *Yes,* Melinda says,
        we can teach you and Henry how to sign.
She makes the same hand movement
    Audrey made, and that's how Molly learns
        her first sign—which means, *Yes.*

BROTHER. SISTER. HOME.

Each time Molly goes to the post office,
    she learns another sign or two:
        Hello. Thank you. Goodbye.
Brother.
    Sister.
        Home.

And at last they receive the letter
    they've been waiting for from Riverview.
        It's official!
Molly signs and says to Audrey and Melinda:
    My brother is coming home! She hopes someone
        has found a way to let Henry know.

Dear Victor,

Have you ever heard of sign language? Well,
it's a way for people to talk by using their hands.
I'm learning it from two sisters, and I have plans
to teach it to Henry when he gets home. Victor, did you tell
one of Henry's friends where we live? We got a letter from
some people whose son told them he was Henry's friend
at Riverview. They have a car—his father said if we send
word, he'll drive us there when Henry is ready to come
home. Mama says that could be as soon as next week!
I hope so! Their son has been teaching them
the card games he and Henry played. They live not far
from here, so they can visit, and if I learn to speak
in sign language, I can interpret for Henry's friend,
so he can talk to Henry. I'm happy! I hope you are.

        Your friend,
        Molly

THREE THINGS

Henry knows three things:
    Ted isn't dead.
    He isn't here.
    He won't be coming back.

It's hard to find new friends.
    I miss the two I had.

A SQUIRREL

When Henry finishes his work,
he sits on his bed and watches
the tree outside the window.
Birds fly above it. A squirrel sits
on a branch with its little paws
in front of it, staring in at Henry.
Maybe it could be my friend, he thinks.
On his way back from breakfast,
he leaves a crust of toast
under the tree, and the squirrel
scampers right over to snatch it up.
Henry smiles. But he misses Ted.

EMPTY PAPER SACK

AUGUST 30, 1944

Victor brings a deck of cards and teaches
Henry how to do a trick: the same card
keeps popping up out of the deck,
even after he mixes them all up.
    Henry watches like a hawk.

He smiles big when he learns how to do it,
but then it makes his loneliness—
his missing—even harder. He wants to show
this trick to Ted. To Billy.
    To Molly and his parents.

He's sitting on his bed,
practicing the trick, pretending
he is showing it to someone, when
he looks out the window,
    and there's the squirrel,

looking in at him, and then it turns
and scampers down the tree trunk. Henry
watches as it runs across the grass and . . .
wait . . . *Isn't that the same car that came*
    the day Ted went away?

Maybe Ted is coming back. At first, Henry
is happy, holding Victor's cards, thinking, *Now
I can show this trick to Ted.* But right away
he thinks, *Oh no. Does he have to come back here?*
    Why can't he stay at home?

Henry is certain the man who gets out
of the car is Ted's father, but who is that
opening the other door? He looks like Papa.
It *is* Papa! And—what? That is Molly
    getting out of the back seat!

Then Victor comes in, smiling, with clean clothes,
and Henry knows what that means. Visitors.
Family! But when Victor puts an empty
paper sack on Henry's bed, and opens it,
    Henry does not understand.

Victor starts putting Henry's things into
the sack. Not much: his drawings,
his tablet, a few broken crayons. The socks
Mama made. His stones and feathers.
    What is going on? he asks.

Victor points out the window
at the three people, now walking up the sidewalk,
straight to this building: Ted's father. Papa. Molly.
Victor says and gestures: *Come on, Henry.*
    Time to go.

THIS IS THE ROAD

Molly has been thinking about how
    to explain all this to Henry. She's drawn
        a picture-map with Riverview on one edge,
        home on the other, a curving gray line

between them: *This is the road,* she'll show
    him. As they drove to Riverview she drew
        whatever she thought Henry might remember:
        the tall water tower near their house,

the first bridge across the river, one
    city, four small towns. The old red
        barn just down the road from Riverview.
        Now, here comes Henry, looking happy

and confused.

He stares at his friend's father, who is talking to Victor.
    Molly wishes she and Henry already knew sign language
        so she could tell him what she hears:
        My son is doing just fine, but he misses Henry.

Molly shows her map to Henry. She points
   first to the real road, then to the line
      on the map. They can see the old red barn
      from here. Molly shows the barn to Henry

on the map she's drawn. Papa puts Henry's
   sack in the car, and Molly runs her finger
      along the map road leading home. Henry
      doesn't dare believe his eyes, until Molly opens

the car door and stretches out her hand. *I can get in?*
   Henry asks. Molly nods. Henry looks at Victor
      to be sure this is okay. Victor smiles and nods,
      then comes to say goodbye. He has a small gift

for Henry—the deck of cards he's shuffled
   so many times the edges are worn and gray. Henry
      isn't sure he should accept it—what will Victor
      do at night when the boys are sleeping?

But he understands the meaning of this gift:
   We will miss each other, won't we? He keeps it
      and gets in the car. Then Victor and Molly talk
      together for a little while. *(Smile, smile, smile.)*

Finally, everyone but Victor is in the car.
    The two fathers sit in front; Molly
        is in back with Henry. They wave goodbye
        to Victor, and drive away from Riverview.

PART III

HOME

1944–1945

CURVY ROAD

AUGUST 30, 1944

Henry looks out the window as the car
    goes down the curvy road. So many houses,
        so many cars. Cows and horses. Another town.

They stop in a small town for lunch. Henry
    can't stop staring at all the different people,
        wearing clothes that aren't gray-green,
or blue, or white—it's hard to tell who's who
    out here. Ted's father leads the way into a place
        where people come in and sit at tables
and someone brings them food. It seems like
    Papa wants him to choose something to eat,
        but how is he supposed to know what food
he wants, or how to ask for it?
    Molly helps him out. She points to soup
        a man is eating at another table—
her eyebrows go up, so Henry sees she's asking
    him if that is what he wants. *Yes,* he nods,
        and soon a lady brings it to him.

Back in the car, Henry's stomach hurts.
    He thinks he might throw up, and then
        he does. He tries not to, but he just can't help it.
Molly sees what's happening. She has a sweater

in her lap and quickly holds it out so he doesn't
      mess up Ted's father's car. Henry is embarrassed,
but Papa puts his hands up in a way that
      Henry understands to mean, *It can happen to anyone.*
         It's not your fault. But still—Molly's sweater
smells like Riverview on a bad day,
      and Henry wants to leave
         that smell behind.

They stop the car. Papa takes Henry
      into a room with toilets and a row of sinks.
         He washes up and rinses out his mouth,
then goes outside and walks around
      until he feels okay. When they get back to the car,
         Molly shows Henry that she's washed her sweater—
it's still wet, but now it doesn't stink.
      Papa gets in the back seat with Molly
         and lets Henry sit in front.

After that, Ted's father drives more slowly.
   Henry can see the curves ahead, and he doesn't
      get sick again. Still, he wishes they'd get home.
He sees a white church he remembers, then
   the water tower . . . the oak tree on the corner.
         There's the place we used to go to mail our letters,
         and the house where we visited the Graysons.
They turn the corner and Henry sees
   what he's been looking for—home!
      And yes—here is Mama.

A SPECIAL DINNER

Mama embraces Henry, smiling and crying.
    She holds him out at arm's length to get
        a good look at him, then pulls him back in
for another hug before they go inside.
    Henry pauses at the kitchen door. He closes
        his eyes to sort out what he smells:
Bread, fresh from the oven. Sweet potatoes.
    Ham or bacon. Apple pie? A bouquet of roses.
        Sawdust. Bleach. Then something he can't name.
It reminds him of Riverview in a good way, but he can't
    quite place it. He opens his eyes and looks around.
        Who? It's true! Ted is standing there, smiling
at him—what is he doing here? The woman behind him
    must be his mother. Mama says something
        and everyone follows her into the other room,
where there are chairs so they can all sit down.
    Ted gets out a drawing—like the ones Henry has seen
        so many times before. His family. Ted points out
his mother in the picture and in the room.
    He does the same for his father, and moves
        his hand to look like someone driving.
It makes sense: Ted and his parents drove to Henry's house.
    Then his father took Papa and Molly to Riverview
        while Ted and his mother stayed here.

According to what Henry smells,
    they helped Mama cook a special dinner
        to say: *Welcome home.*

Dear Victor,

You asked me to write a note to let you know
we made it safely home. It was a nice trip—not
uneventful (Henry was carsick), but, yes, we got
home in time for dinner. I wish I could show
you the look on Henry's face when he saw his friend.
He was confused at first, but they were so happy to see
each other. Henry got out the cards you gave him and we
all learned a game both boys knew. Next weekend,
we've planned that they will come here to pick us
up and drive us to their house, over in the next town.
We're glad the boys can see each other. How's everything for
you, Victor? I'm glad I had a chance to meet you. I just
wish you could get out of that place too. Please come down
and see us, even if you have to wait until after the war.

Your friend,
Molly

ALL HE KNEW

Henry is drawing, remembering all he knew
  of home: the table with different kinds of food,
    his family all together, the trees outside—
so big now, blackberries almost ripe.
  Even after five long years, Snowball
    recognizes Henry, and rubs against his ankles.

Sometimes Henry draws what he remembers
  from Riverview: baby birds in a nest
    and the squirrel in the tree outside
the broken window. A row of boys strapped
  into chairs. A broken sink. Tables with benches.
    Billy's grave. Appleman. Victor. Molly recognizes
Victor—Henry is really good at drawing.
  She shows him the envelope with her letter
    to Victor, then points to Henry's picture of him,
and to the pile of the other pictures
  he has drawn. She raises her eyebrows
    in a question, so Henry chooses two pictures:
his family sitting at the table, and the squirrel
  at Riverview. He folds them and puts them into
    Molly's envelope for her to send to Victor.
Molly smiles and nods and makes the sign
  that Audrey and Melinda taught her. *Yes.*
    They understand each other as they always have.

HENRY FEELS BRAVE

Molly points out the post office
    on the map she's drawn.
    Come with me, she gestures,
        opening the front door for Henry.

He's not sure he wants to go.
    It's been a long time since he's talked
    to people who don't know him.
        If he tries, will they understand him?

Old memories surface. Big boys teasing
    Molly about him. Sadie in tears.
    Can people tell by looking at me, he wonders,
        that I can't hear what they're saying?

He hates that look
    when a person he meets seems to know
    there's something different about him,
        and they aren't sure what it is.

Still, he does like
    being with his sister.
    And he wants to look around.
        Okay, he says, *I'll try.*

Molly writes something on a card
    and gives it to him, pointing to his pocket.
    He doesn't know it says, *Hello, my name*
        is Henry, but he puts it in his pocket anyway.

He feels brave when he steps
    out the door with Molly. Most people
    smile at them as they walk downtown,
        and Henry smiles back.

LOTS OF US

Inside the post office, Molly shows him
    how to buy a stamp, put it on a letter,
      and give the letter to the man behind the counter.
        Henry remembers some of this.

Molly waves at two women
    working in the back. They see her
    and come over to where she and Henry
      stand. Molly touches Henry's shoulder.

He looks at her and she points to his pocket, makes
    the shape of the card with her hands.
    Henry takes out the card and offers it
      to Molly, but she gestures toward the women.

Henry gives the card to one of them.
    She smiles. Henry hopes these women
    won't try to talk to him—at first, they don't.
      Then one woman raises her hand to her forehead.

The other one does the exact same thing,
    and Molly does it too. They all look
    at Henry, so he tries doing what they did.
      The two women and Molly smile.

It brings back a memory to Henry:
   how it felt when he was little,
   when someone talked to him
      and he could hear them.

Something begins to dawn on Henry.
   He points to his own ears, then to
   Audrey's, with a question on his face,
      and she nods and signs, *Yes.*

He points to Melinda, and Audrey
   shakes her head, *No.* Henry understands
   that Audrey is deaf, like him.
      Melinda hears, like Molly.

I thought I was the only one, he says.
   Melinda interprets that for Audrey,
   who smiles at Henry and says,
      in words and signs, *There are lots of us.*

She puts her hand on Henry's shoulder,
   and he lets it stay there
   as he looks down at the ground,
   holding back a sudden rush of tears.

LIKE A TREE

Henry watches Molly say something
    to Melinda, who signs to Audrey.
        They both smile at Henry. Molly writes
something on a card and gives it to them.
    Audrey puts the card in her pocket,
        and the two sisters go back to work.

The next day, Henry and Molly are out
    in their garden, when Audrey and Melinda
        come walking up the street, looking at
their card and at the numbers on the houses.
    Molly goes to meet them and invite them
        to come in for lemonade.

She gets out Henry's drawings
    and puts them on the table.
        Melinda picks up his picture of a tree.
Audrey bends one arm, holds it flat
    and puts her other elbow on the back
        of her hand. She holds her fingers up,

waves them in the air, and smiles.
    Like a tree and its leaves, Henry sees.
        He points out the window at the apple tree.

Melinda nods, and Audrey makes the same
    sign again. Henry is thinking hard. He points
       to a different tree and makes the tree

sign with his hands. He puts his eyebrows up
    to ask: *Is this how you say* tree?
       Audrey makes a fist, holds it up,
and gently moves it up and down.
    Henry understands that she is saying,
       Yes.

SIGN LANGUAGE

Audrey and Melinda stop by
    every afternoon on their way home
        from the post office. After each visit,
Henry and Molly know a few more signs:
    Thank you. You're welcome. Would you like:
        Food? Water? These flowers? This picture?
Henry draws pictures and they show him
    how to talk about them, using signs.
        Mama and Papa try to learn
along with them, but they're not quite so quick,
    and it's not long before their children
        can tell secrets right in front of them.

Dear Molly,

Thank you for that good letter. I do miss
both those boys, but I'm very glad
to know they're home and that they've had
a chance to get together. As you know, this
place is overcrowded, and some of the boys
unfortunately come from homes they can't go back
to. We'd like it to be more of a real home, but we lack
funds for decent food, to say nothing of toys
for the younger ones, warm clothing, boots, shoes.
Surely America can do better. Is it really asking so
much, to treat all people as we'd each want to be
treated ourselves? This endless war is no excuse
for keeping people locked up when they've done no
wrong. I suppose I am ranting. Forgive me.

Your friend,
Victor

Dear Victor,

Molly is teaching me to read
and write. It is hard.
You know that card
that has a king on it? You need
to know that K *means* king
and the other one, Q,
means queen. *Then you*
look for something
else with the same
letter. I found out that my
friend's name is not
Ted. It is Ned. But your name
is really Victor. Just like I
always thought.

> *Your friend,*
> *Henry*

Dear Victor,

It is amazing how fast Henry is learning to sign
and spell. I enclose a letter he wrote to you
with very little help. He wants to send a drawing, too.
I think it's very good—much better than any of mine.
We are hoping you can visit. If you get some days
off, and can take the bus here, you will be most
welcome. My parents have offered to host
Ned's family for Thanksgiving, and his father says
to let you know that if you could join us he'll drive you
back to Riverview after dinner. Let us know if you can come.
My school is collecting winter coats and canned food
for Riverview, and we could send them then. (Too
costly to mail.) You'll see that this is a humble home,
but my mother's (and Ned's mother's) cooking is good!

Your friend,
Molly

OCTOBER 29, 1944

Dear Molly and Henry,

I enjoyed reading your letters! Henry, your
picture of the tree outside our window looks a lot
like the tree itself, with that little squirrel—not
scampering around, but peeking in, looking for
all the world like it's your best friend. I know
it would be proud of you. I am! You are very kind
to invite me for Thanksgiving. Would you mind
if my parents and brother joined us? They are so
far away from Riverview, and you (and Ned) live
about halfway. I'd like Ned to see how my father
gets along with just one arm. My parents will share
any food they have from their garden, and they'll give
you ration tickets. If that would not be too much bother,
please let me know. I look forward to visiting you there.

Your friend,
Victor

ONE BIG TABLE

THANKSGIVING 1944

Papa brings four sawhorses inside
    and puts boards on top of them. Mama sews
        two sheets together to make a tablecloth
so it looks like one big table, which Molly sets
    for everyone. Henry and Papa make a bench.
        Audrey and Melinda will bring two extra chairs.
Mama asks Molly to go outside
    and cut greens for a centerpiece,
        and Molly asks, by signing,
Henry, do you want to help?
    He says and signs back to her,
        Yes, I'm coming.
Outdoors, the air is crisp and cool. Molly cuts
    the branches and Henry holds them in his arms—
        they smell just like they look.
Green. Fresh. Clean.
    Henry closes his eyes
        and breathes.

AROUND THE TABLE

Henry draws a picture of each person on a folded card.
    Molly writes their names and they put them around
        the table: Papa at one end, Henry at the corner
next to Papa, then Ned, his three sisters, and his parents.
    Mama and Molly at the end near the kitchen, Victor
        next to Molly, then his brother Joey,
and their parents. They put Audrey and Melinda
    close to Henry so he can talk to them
        more easily, and maybe learn a few new signs.
Mama looks around the room, pleased with
    how it looks. A memory comes: those two
        dressed-up ladies long ago. *Our home,*
she thinks, *is a proper place*
    to raise a child like this.
        Henry. A child like Henry—
        thoughtful, kind, and smart.

FRIENDS ALREADY

They're coming! They're coming!
   They're almost here! says Henry.
      They're here! Victor and his family arrive
at almost the same time, on two different buses
   from opposite directions. Henry feels shy
      all of a sudden, but Victor's mother smiles
in that way some people have
   that makes you relax and smile back.
      I'm Emma Jorgensen, she says, adding,
Victor's mother. Although Henry doesn't hear the words,
   it's obvious: She can't stop looking at her son.
      And this—she seems proud to say—*is my husband, Ollie.*
As in Victor's picture, his father is missing one arm.
   Henry wonders if he'll find out how that happened.
      A car drives up: Ted—*no,* Henry remembers, *his name
is Ned.* More introductions that Henry understands
   by watching closely. He wonders what Victor's father
      is saying to Ned about his empty sleeve. He asks Molly
if she can tell him using signs, and she says, *I'll try.*
   She listens carefully and thinks hard, then signs,
      He was in a war when he was young.
He doesn't know exactly how it happened.
   He didn't think Emma would marry him, but she did.
      (Victor's mother smiles, and so does Ned,

222

when Victor's father says that.)
    Now Victor's older brother is in this war.
        They hope all the soldiers will come home soon.

The Bradley sisters walk up the street
    carrying their chairs. Henry, Ned, and Molly
        run out to help. Now everyone is here, and happy.

Victor and Molly keep smiling
    at each other, until Molly has to go
        help Mama in the kitchen.
Then Victor turns to Ned and Henry,
    gets out a brand new deck of cards, and shows
        them a trick he's been practicing. Ned's
little sisters watch six times and still can't see
    how Victor does it. Henry figures it out
        the second time (so easy!), and Ned the third.
Victor's brother Joey must have learned the trick before—
    maybe he's the one who teaches tricks to Victor.
        Henry looks around: *So many people*
in this little house, he thinks,
    and I'm the one
        who brought us all together.

HENRY SMELLS CINNAMON

The four families have pooled
    their food and ration tickets
        to come up with this feast.
Roast chicken,
    mashed potatoes, gravy, apple pie
        with sugar sprinkled on it.
Henry smells something delicious, and
    somewhere deep in his mind, he finds
        the word that lets him name it.
Cinnamon, he says. Audrey and Melinda
    show him how to sign it, and then
        everyone wants to learn that sign.

They sit down and bow their heads. Henry remembers
    what they used to say: *Come, Lord Jesus, be our guest . . .*
        That's what they must be saying now, so he joins in.

The conversation moves around the table,
    reminding Henry of how birds fly in the sky, then
        land on a treetop before taking off again, one after another.

When Molly is talking, everyone looks at her,
    and when she stops, Henry watches where everyone
        looks next, and that's how he knows who answers.

He sees how Melinda listens and then signs
    to Audrey, and after Audrey signs, Melinda talks
        and everyone else listens to her. Henry can
tell when she's talking for herself and when
    she is interpreting for Audrey, and he is filled
        with happiness to see how this can work.

Victor says something that makes everyone look
    at Ned and Henry. Both their mothers' eyes
        brim with tears, then blaze with anger.
Mama stands and leaves the room.
    Henry doesn't think she's mad at Victor,
        or at anyone who's sitting here today.
When Melinda interprets the conversation,
    Audrey looks the same as Mama did.
        Henry understands that Victor told them
something about Riverview that was unfair, or cruel.
    If they just found out how Ned was treated,
        Henry is glad it made them mad.

I'll keep learning how to read and write, he thinks,
    and someday I'll tell people what that place
        is like. It doesn't have to be the way it is.

Dear Mr. and Mrs. Williams, Molly, and Henry,

Thank you for including me and my family in your
Thanksgiving gathering. We very much enjoyed
the food and fellowship, and it buoyed
my spirits more than I can tell you. More
than I knew I needed. I want to let you know—
of all the boys at Riverview, Henry and Ned
were the first to be discharged. Maybe you have read
about the changes here—it's been in the papers. There are so
many others who should not be here. There is a lot at stake—
boys like yours are helpful, and we need that help—but along
with the other COs, I am insisting that we have no right
to keep anyone at Riverview because the work they do may make
our own lives easier. My visit with you made these strong
feelings even stronger, and that helps me keep up this fight.

Your friend,

Victor

VICTOR HAS A QUESTION

MAY 1945

For the second time since Thanksgiving,
    Victor takes the Greyhound bus
        to visit Henry's family. (Henry
is beginning to wonder: Is it him or Molly
    Victor loves to visit?) Each time he comes, they
        can have a better conversation,
because Henry is talking more freely now,
    and Molly can interpret what Victor says
        so Henry can understand and answer him.
This time, Victor has good news:
    My brother Steven has come home, he says.
        A lot of hard things happened to him, but he's
alive and he is safe now. They're saying we can hope that
    all the fighting will be over soon. Molly signs
        all this to Henry and he says, *I'm glad your brother*
came back, Victor. He thinks about how happy he was
    when he got out of Riverview, and how he would feel
        if Molly were in danger and then she came home safe.
They're quiet for a moment. Then Victor has a question.
    Molly, he begins, *there's something I have always*
        wanted to ask Henry. Can you interpret for us?
Molly agrees to try, and Victor explains:
    On my first day at Riverview, I left a book
        wedged in a door, to hold it open. It was very early,

and I thought all the boys were sleeping.
  Molly does her best to sign this to Henry,
    and he answers, *Yes, I remember that.*
Victor goes on: *Do you remember your little friend*
    who died? Henry says, *Yes, of course I remember Billy.*
    Victor and Molly are confused—the boy
was named Buddy. They think about it, and say
    the two names—if Henry was trying
      to lip-read, *Buddy* might look a lot like
Billy. The same reason he thought *Ned*
    was *Ted.* Henry understands that he has
      another name wrong, but that is not
what matters most right now.
  What about that book? he asks, and Victor
    goes on: *I was supposed to count the boys*
when we went to breakfast, and again
    when we got back to the ward.
      My breakfast count was two boys short.
I thought I'd made a terrible mistake.
    Did I have the numbers wrong?
      Should I report two missing children?
Which ones? I didn't yet know who was who—you all wore
    the same color clothes. If two children were missing,
      I'd be fired. I was afraid I'd be sent to prison.
He stops again, and Molly signs as much as she can
    to Henry. He doesn't understand the part about prison.
      That's hard to explain, Victor says—*I am working*
at Riverview because I will not participate in war.

If I couldn't do that work, they'd lock me up, to keep me
    from spreading my beliefs to others. Henry remembers
when Slim Jim and Barker pushed Victor down
    and spit on him. *Was that the reason?* he asks. *Yes,*
        says Victor. Henry thinks about that. Then he returns
to Victor's question. *Billy—Buddy—got outside that morning;*
    I woke up early and saw him on the road
        all by himself. So I went out after him.
I found him hiding in that old red barn. He was scared.
    I was scared. I brought him back to Riverview,
        but I didn't know how we'd get back inside
without being caught and punished. Then I saw the line
    of boys walking to breakfast, and we slipped in at the end.
        That was the first day I met you, Victor. You were nice.
You didn't strap us down or hit us. Molly gets the same look
    on her face as Henry's and Ned's mothers had
        when Victor told them about Riverview.
Thank you, Henry says to Victor, who shakes his head.
    No, he says, *thank* you, *Henry. You taught me to be careful.*
        No books holding doors open—no shortcuts on safety rules.
Molly interprets this, looking from her brother to
    the young man she has come to care for, though
        it will be several years before she tells him so.

As I understand this, she says and signs,
    you saved each other.
        Victor nods and says, *Yes, we did.*
Henry adds, *You helped us, Molly.*

The three of them are smiling now.
They understand each other
perfectly.

THE NICEST BOY

JUNE, 1945

Henry and Molly are out in their front yard
    when a girl about Henry's age walks by. She stops
        and looks at him and breaks into a big smile.
Henry? she says, *Is that you? You're back?*
    He has to look twice before he recognizes her—could this
        be Sadie? *Hello, Sadie,* he says. He's decided to try
talking to people, explaining like he did with Ned:
    I can talk, but I can't hear. When you talk to me,
        look right at me and speak clearly. Molly can help
by using sign language when we need her.
        Sadie still talks a lot, but she listens too. She wants to know
            all about sign language and Riverview and Ned and Victor.
Henry doesn't tell her everything—he doesn't want to make her sad.
        And he has questions too: what's it like to be eleven years old here,
            almost twelve? Sadie talks long and fast. It sounds to Henry
like she wants to be friends again. *If you have*
        another birthday party, I'll ask my mother
            to make another cake, and this time, I'll only throw
the ball to you, not to those boys that wouldn't let me play.
        That way, I won't break your window. Henry still doesn't
            know what happened that day, so Sadie explains it,
and when Molly interprets, Henry laughs and then
        so does Sadie. *We were so little,* she says. Henry
            answers, *So were those other boys, Sadie.*

People can get nicer. If they want to play catch
  with us, we can let them. Sadie looks at him
     and thinks about that. Then she says, so carefully
they don't need an interpreter, *I remember*
  you were the nicest boy. I've missed you, Henry.
     I'm glad you're back.

NOTES ON FORM AND CHARACTERS

FORM

Most of these poems are in free verse, with lines and stanzas arranged on the page in ways that vary from poem to poem.

The letter poems, set in italics, and other poems telling Victor's part of the story, are sonnets, using elements of several variations of the sonnet form. Each poem has fourteen lines, with the end words of the lines rhyming in this order: *abba cddc efgefg*, where each letter represents a rhyme. Some rhymes are not exact, but there is always an echo of at least one sound or visual element.

The sequence of poems titled "The Middle Brother" is a crown of sonnets—the last line of one sonnet is the first line of the next, usually slightly altered, and the last line of the last sonnet in the crown circles back to the first line of the first one.

CHARACTERS

The children at Riverview face different challenges. Billy (Buddy) has what is today called Down syndrome or trisomy 21. Ted (Ned) has cerebral palsy. At the time this story takes place, children with many different disabilities were often moved out of their homes and placed in institutions where they did not receive the kind of care and education they needed and deserved.

In imagining Victor, I was deeply influenced by the book *Down in My Heart*, William Stafford's memoir of his World War II service as a conscientious objector, and by *The Turning Point*, Alex Sareyan's nonfiction chronicle of the experience of conscientious objectors who served in institutions such as Riverview during that same war.

Victor's parents, Emma and Oliver (Ollie) Jorgensen, and his Aunt Muriel first appeared as teenagers in my book *Crossing Stones*.

AUTHOR'S NOTE

Soon after I met my husband and his family in the early 1980s, I learned of his mother's brother Shirley Sowers, who lived from 1904 to 1969. (Shirley was a boy's name, as well as a girl's name, in 1904.) I'm not sure if he was born deaf, or if he lost his hearing due to an illness at a young age. Because the family was not wealthy, and teachers in the small town where he lived did not know how to teach deaf children, Shirley was mislabeled "unteachable" and sent to live in an institution for the "feebleminded," where, a few years later, he had an accident in which he lost most (possibly all) of his eyesight. Those who knew him best, including his sister Maxine (my husband's mother), recall that he never lost his intelligence or loving nature.

Maxine began writing poems about her brother and sharing them with me. She wrote one or two poems a year for several years, and when she had sent seven of them, she said she was finished, adding, "The only reason I ever wanted to write poetry was to give my brother the life he never had." We compiled the poems in a small book, *The Unteachable One*, and printed about 150 copies for friends and family.

I often thought about the story told in these seven poems, and wondered if I could find a way to write about something similar that would be engaging and meaningful to children living today. Would anyone believe that at one time a child could be moved out of his home and never receive an education simply because he was deaf and did not speak? Shirley Sowers lived in institutions for the rest of his life, but I imagined the life a child might have had if he had been born a few decades later, in slightly different circumstances, and could speak if he chose to do so.

I have also been thinking for many years about the Americans who, for reasons of conscience, did not take part in World War II. Most Americans believed the war was just and necessary, and there was a draft, which meant that young men were required to register for military service and serve if called upon to do so. But as there are in every war, there were conscientious objectors—people who took a stand for peace by refusing to participate in the war.

About twelve thousand people held religious beliefs or other moral convictions that led them to refuse World War II military service. The United States government placed many of them in Civilian Public Service (CPS) jobs— nonmilitary work that was important and necessary for the good of the country. They were essentially volunteers, being paid as little as $2.50 per month and enduring long periods of separation from their families and communities. Some, but not all, received financial support from their religious communities.

Of the twelve thousand CPS workers, about three thousand were assigned to work as attendants in state hospitals and training centers. Riverview is fictional; I have chosen not to set the story in a specific place, because I don't want it to be about any one institution—the conditions I have depicted reflect what life was like in many institutions at that time. I have also not named Victor's specific religion. The CPS workers included people from many different faiths, as well as people who were not religious. About half were from churches known as historic peace churches—Amish, Church of the Brethren, Mennonite, and Quaker.

The conscientious objectors were often called (and called themselves) COs. Many Americans of that time despised them, thinking they were cowardly and unpatriotic. Some people used the insulting term conchies to describe them. In actuality, the COs were as brave and patriotic in their own way as those who served in the military, and their work for peace was of great benefit to the country.

Institutions for people with psychiatric or intellectual disabilities were severely understaffed during the years of World War II. Many people who worked in them left their jobs for military service, or to take higher-paying jobs that became available when others enlisted. Because there were not enough attendants in the institutions, the government assigned conscientious objectors to do that work.

Most of the institutions were bleak places to begin with, and the shortage of attendants made them worse. The COs brought a spirit of love and respect to the people in their care, which, not surprisingly, had a positive effect. Change was slow, but it did come, and it continued after the war was over. Deep thinking about the right of all people to be treated fairly, including the right to receive an equal education, contributed to the passage of the Civil Rights Act in 1964 and, eventually, to the Americans with Disabilities Act in 1990.

Today there are many ways to teach and communicate with d/Deaf children, and it is not legal to deny them an equal education. A word of explanation: The word *deaf* is sometimes, but not always, capitalized. When written with a lowercase *d*, *deaf* refers to the audiological condition of not hearing. Capitalized, *Deaf* means a particular group of deaf people who share a culture and a language—American Sign Language or another signed language.

I have heard about many children born before the 1970s who were thought to be "unteachable" (or "ineducable") and thus did not receive the education they deserved. Each of those stories has its own specific details. I adapted the blowing-out-a-match test that Maxine remembered, although that has never been a standard way of testing children.

Maxine Sowers Thompson did not live to see the publication of this book, but on the following pages, with permission of her family, I share with you her seven poems—*The Unteachable One*. In a poignant moment described in the sixth poem, you will meet Maxine and Shirley's brother, who really was named Ted.

THE UNTEACHABLE ONE

BY MAXINE THOMPSON

Dedicated to the memory
of my brother
Shirley Sowers
1904–1969

THE UNTEACHABLE ONE

A small child in nightgown stands
In the kitchen doorway, her bare feet cold
On the wide board flooring.
Darkness is behind her, darkness is upstairs,
Darkness fills the night outside.

A kerosene lamp lights the kitchen
Casting shadows on walls and ceiling.
Ghosts they are, sitting at the kitchen table,
The mother with her deaf-mute son.
She lights matches—he blows them out,
One after one without faltering.
Why is she crying?

In a far-off time, at a faraway school
They said, "He cannot be taught,
He didn't blow out the matches."
She pleaded, "He's frightened.
He's never been away from home."
They repeated, "He cannot be taught.
He failed the test."
The mother cuddles the child.
The boy watches the flame.
And there they sit,
Frozen in time and memory.

THE UNTEACHABLES

Against the long white wall
Of the institution
Are the straight-back chairs
Where sit the mutes and mindless alike,
Not for a day or a year,
But for a lifetime.
They wait there for the kiss
That permits them to leave
And go where earth
Enfolds them gently.

LETTERS COME

Palls of gloom from the institution
Come in long white envelopes.
They begin, "We regret to say
Your son is ill." Or, "He has the flu."
Once it read, "He fell today and lost an eye,
Maybe two. We'll let you know."

With children home and being poor,
The mother knows no way to go
To hold him close or stroke his brow.
She walks the floor. She weeps.
The children cry. They don't know why.

HER FIRST VISIT

Blithe, full of life, his sister
Now at the door of teens
Brings treats of apples, oranges,
And wintergreens to him
She hasn't seen since she was four.

The attendant says, "Stay here.
I'll bring the boy to you."
She follows anyway,
A thing she shouldn't do.

In chairs they sit, dressed alike
In garbs of faded blue.
Some roaring, some swaying,
Or quietly waiting, but staying
As they are supposed to do.

She turns away in sorrow.
Gone, gone her joy.
If she could, she would
Erase the scene that parades
Across her screen of memory.

THE ORANGE

He doesn't hear, he barely sees,
But seems to know who's there.
His trembling hand he holds out,
No doubt to ask for treats.

A golden orange,
Thick-skinned and sweet,
He neatly sections
And eagerly begins to eat.

His sister weeps.
Sensing something wrong,
He stops and waits,
Then offers her his orange.

When Moses' rod smote the rock,
Water did appear.
The orange, like Moses' rod,
Smote her heart,
Brought forth instead
An artesian well of tears.

THE VICTORY

The arc of time
Spans fifty years and more
Yet he knows the brother
Who played with him
But has never come before.

Though death stands near,
He, white and gaunt on his bed,
Turns his head toward the door,
Raises a hand and grins
An open-mouth grin,
Something we'd not seen before.

More than joy,
More than elation.
Ours was silent awe
Of his communication.

THE GIFT

In a suit for the first time ever,
He looked like a little old professor
Asleep in his coffin, lying on his side.
They didn't want to break his legs
So they left him curled as he had died.

Kinder to him than life, death
Raised the veil of infirmities
From his face, and in their place
Intelligence was left for all to see.
Oh, the joy of this act of grace!

Who fills his chair
Left empty there against the wall
Where others sit and wait
the call that sets them free to go
To nourish earth that nourished them,
Their ultimate gift to life.

ACKNOWLEDGMENTS

One day, as I was deep in the process of learning about and imagining the setting for this story, I drove with a friend to the abandoned site of a state hospital, something like Riverview may have been. We walked around the grounds for about an hour and I thought about the thousands of people who lived and died in such institutions. Let me begin by acknowledging the significance and dignity of their lives.

In writing this book, I have had many helpful guides and companions. As I thank them, I wish to note that any remaining errors are entirely my own.

Willy Conley, a Deaf poet, professor, photographer, and dramatist, who teaches at Gallaudet University, advised me in the kindest, most helpful ways as I imagined Henry's experience. His novel, *The Deaf Heart*, is informative, beautiful, and engaging. Thank you, Willy.

In finding information I needed, I was lucky to have access to the Allen County Public Library's excellent collection of books and materials. And I thank Carrie Phillips, archivist at Bluffton University, who helped me find records of World War II conscientious objectors who served in state hospitals.

Poetry has sustained me in countless ways. I thank the children's poetry community, as well as poets who write for adults. For this book, I am especially indebted to

Christianne Balk, Willy Conley, Jeff Gundy, Ann Hostetler, Marc Hudson, Don Mager, Kim Stafford, William Stafford, and Ingrid Wendt. I am grateful for permission to include the epigraph from William Stafford's beautiful poem "At the Un-National Monument Along the Canadian Border."

In addition to these writers, I thank other friends who have devoted many years to working for peace, often including conscientious objection to war. To name just a few: John and Beth Murphy Beams, Ketu Oladuwa, Sox Sperry, and Lisa Tsetse.

Al Rath, my great-uncle, was a conscientious objector in World War II, serving as an attendant in a psychiatric institution and working for the rest of his life to bring about changes that began in those years. His daughter Jane Rath Dickie and her husband, Larry, along with Jane's sisters, Linda and Nancy, were helpful and encouraging.

Many friends have shared experiences that helped me tell this story. Leslie Bracebridge has worked for decades making homes for women who were released as institutions closed down. Maureen Binienda taught her brother to read when others questioned whether he could learn; he is still a reader today, and Maureen has gone on to become a remarkable educator, beginning as a special education teacher and now serving as superintendent of a large school district. Ruth Langhinrichs, near the end of her life, at age ninety-five, shared her memories of working in a state institution during World War II, and her story of dating a conscientious objector whose mother told her not to marry him because even the young man's mother felt that his being a CO was shameful.

Sharon Verbeten, Christianne Balk, and Helen Hudson all read the manuscript and helped me think about the families of children whose care requires extra time, devotion, and resources. Crystal Arreguin and her ASL interpreter, Brittany Foldes, made time for a very helpful conversation during my visit to Fischer Middle School in Aurora, Illinois. Ed Spicer shared valuable insights about the portrayal of deafness in children's literature. I'm grateful for the decades-long friendship of Steve and Susan Harroff and Dan and Diane Schmucker.

Thanks to Ginger Knowlton and others at Curtis Brown for finding the right home for my manuscript, and to everyone at FSG/Macmillan for making it into a beautiful book. Special thanks to Janine O'Malley and Melissa Warten for careful and perceptive editing; copyeditor Karen Sherman and production editor Mandy Veloso; cover artist Pascal Campion and book designer Cassie Gonzales. Thank you, Kelsey Marrujo, Lucy Del Priore, and others who helped the finished book find its way into the hands of readers. And thanks to Kate Kubert Puls for helping me meet many of those readers.

I continue to appreciate the support of the Authors Guild and the Society of Children's Book Writers and Illustrators (SCBWI), especially the Indiana listserv and the Fort Wayne critique group. Thanks to real life friends and those on social media for ongoing conversations and encouragement.

I am deeply grateful to my husband and his family, especially his mother, Maxine Thompson, and his sisters, Margaret, Jane, and Sarah, for sharing their memories of Shirley Sowers, and for granting permission to include *The Unteachable One* in this book.

Thanks to my sisters and brothers and their families, my stepson, Lloyd, and his wife, Anastacia, and my son, Glen.

As always, thank you, Chad, for insight, patience, support, great cooking, and beautiful music.

HELEN FROST is the author of many books for young people, including *When My Sister Started Kissing, Salt, Hidden, Diamond Willow, Crossing Stones, The Braid*, and *Keesha's House*, selected as an Honor Book for the Michael L. Printz Award. Ms. Frost lives in Fort Wayne, Indiana. **helenfrost.net**

A NOTE ON THE TYPE

The main text of this book is set in ITC Legacy Serif, a typeface designed by American designer Ronald Arnholm. He began working in 1982 and released the typeface in 1993. ITC Legacy Serif is a revival and reinterpretation of Nicolas Jenson's original roman style typeface, created for the 1470 print edition of *Eusebius*. Jenson's roman style did not include an italic, so Arnholm referenced sixteenth-century designs by Claude Garamond to form the base of the italic weight. ITC Legacy Serif is practical and highly legible due to its open counters and clean forms. These typographic features allow the spare lines of poetry to sit gently on the page.